**BARNEY BUCK AND
THE ROUGH RIDER SPECIAL**

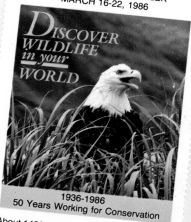

NATIONAL WILDLIFE FEDERATION
NATIONAL WILDLIFE WEEK
MARCH 16-22, 1986

DISCOVER
WILDLIFE
in your
WORLD

1936-1986
50 Years Working for Conservation

About 1400 pairs of bald eagles nest in the
lower 48 states; about 7500 nest in Alaska.

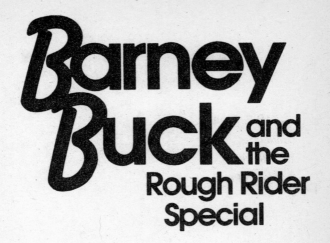

Barney Buck and the Rough Rider Special

GILBERT MORRIS

WindRider BOOKS
Tyndale House Publishers, Inc., Wheaton, Illinois

TO GALE TONEY

*"A friend
sticketh closer
than a brother."*

First printing, November 1985

Library of Congress Catalog Card Number 85-51283
ISBN 0-8423-0134-8

CONTENTS

ONE
Too Much Bull

In a small school like Cedarville High where everybody knew everybody else, when a new kid moved in, he just naturally stirred interest. Usually, though, new people were just about like the rest of us, which made the excitement settle down pretty fast. Until one morning in March, that is.

I was sitting outside the front door with a bunch of kids waiting for old Mr. Clooney to let us in at eight o'clock when suddenly Marilyn Freeman said in a hushed voice, "Who is *that?*"

We all turned to look at a new guy getting out of a fancy CJ-7 Cherokee Jeep with a warn winch, a chrome roll bar, and a set of halogen lights that could probably have burned holes in tool steel. He was around 6'1" and weighed about a hundred ninety pounds with most of it in his upper body like the weight lifters. His hair was so black it made his tan face look almost pale. He wore a white Stetson with a low crown pushed back on his head, jeans, a belt made of snakeskin with a big silver buckle, and lizard-skin boots all scuffed and worn but expensive. His eyes were wide set, dark brown or black, and his mouth was wide with a full lower lip. That was the only thing, I guess, that didn't go with the Hollywood star look. His lower lip was so full he seemed to be pouting. I guess nobody noticed that but me.

Anyway, this cool-looking "dude" ambled along to where we were sitting and stopped. Reaching into his hip pocket, he pulled out a round can of Skoal, pulled out some chewing tobacco, then asked, "Hey, where's the head honcho of this mental institution?"

Marilyn was so paralyzed she couldn't say a word. I got a kick out of that, because she was usually pretty laid back. I gave Debra Simmons a look, but she was staring at the guy as if she'd been hypnotized.

And she wasn't the only one. Every girl in sight was trying hard not to stare at this fellow—and not doing too well at it. I gave Debra a nudge with my elbow to bring her out of it. Then I said, "Principal's office is down the hall to the right—last door. Can't get in until they unlock the door, though."

The newcomer grinned, exposing perfect teeth, and a sigh seemed to go around from the females in the group. "No sweat," he said in a deep voice. "I'm Jack Monroe. Just moved in from Tulsa."

I got up and stuck out my hand. "Barney Buck. That's Marilyn, Gerald French, Al Carter. . . ." I went around the group and wound up with Debra. ". . . And this is Debra Simmons."

"Howdy," he said waving a big hand slightly. "Heck of a time to be changin' schools, ain't it now?" Actually he didn't really say *heck*.

I flinched a little at the way he cussed. Most of our guys watched the way they talked in front of girls. "Only two months left," I answered. "Be kind of hard to get settled in and then leave on vacation."

"Oh, I wanted to quit and go rodeoing, but the old man promised me if I stuck it out he'd buy me a roping horse I got my eye on." He grinned again, and that triggered a little sigh from those silly girls. "I guess you got a little action here, ain't you? I mean, it ain't *Tulsa*, but I guess if we only got one trip around, we gotta live it with all the gusto we can, right?" He looked right at Debra and asked in an *intimate* tone, "What do you do around this burg for excitement?"

The way he moved right in made me mad. He was really saying that he was big time and was going to show us hicks how it should be done. I opened my mouth without thinking. "Well, cowboy," I began, "usually when we want a thrill, we go down to the railroad trestle and throw rocks. But when we really let it *all* hang out, we go down to the barbershop and watch a couple of haircuts."

I knew right away that I'd pay for that wisecrack sooner or later. He didn't say anything at first, but there was a sudden flash of light in his dark eyes and a twitch in his jaw muscles. He smiled and said, "Well, Buck, I can see you lead a real dangerous life." Then he added, "Maybe I can show you how to turn your wolf loose—if you got the guts for it!"

Right then we heard the door open, and Jack went in, but I knew he wouldn't forget me. That's the way it sometimes is with guys. I don't know why. Two fellows meet and it's like two strange dogs. They circle around stiff legged, and everybody knows that sooner or later they'll have it out.

Debra glared at me as we went in. She was pretty good at that—with those dark eyes of hers. "Why'd you have to say that?" she demanded.

"He's a phoney," I said. "Couldn't you tell?"

"No, I couldn't. And I think you're getting pretty *insular!*"

"Insular?" I echoed, pulling her to a stop.

"Yes, *insular!* It means you don't want to accept any new thoughts or people into your own little world."

"I know what it *means*," I snapped. "I don't

agree that it's what I *am*. Did you check out his clothes, Debra? There's something wrong with any guy who wants to play cowboy when he's older than ten, wouldn't you say?"

Actually I wasn't too sure of that, but I was mad. And when I get mad, I say stupid things. I'm still working on it, but not doing too well.

The way it turned out was that the whole school went gaga over the cowboy! I don't mean just the girls—the guys, too. And let me be honest, he wasn't just a drugstore cowboy. We'd had quite a few rodeos around the county, and from what I'd heard, Jack Monroe was about the best bronc rider to hit the state in a while. I wasn't into the horse thing myself, but I had a couple of friends who rodeoed and they said he was *good!*

But I'd made my play, and I guess I was just too proud to back up. Every time anyone said something about Jack Monroe, I made a wisecrack. I knew it was wrong, but to tell the truth, I was upset about the way Debra was buying his bill of goods.

Now she and I weren't going together (whatever that means), but we were *good* friends, and I figured that sooner or later when we got older, we'd have an understanding. But every time I tried to explain this to her, she just tapped her chin with one finger and said, "Hmmmmm."

Now what in the cat hair can you do with a girl who says, "Hmmmm?"

Before long Debra got a horse named Royal, not just any old saddle horse but one trained to run barrels. When she told me her dad had paid four thousand dollars for Royal, I nearly died!

"Why, that would feed a regiment of starving Koreans for a year!" I shouted. "It's—it's immoral!"

"No, it's not!" she snapped right back. We were standing in the corral at her house where she'd been practicing. It was a surprise for me, or was supposed to be. She'd asked me to come after school, and her face was all lit up when she showed me Royal and then did the barrel trick.

Riding the barrels is the big thing for girls in rodeo. The barrels are placed in a triangular position on the field, and then the horse has to circle them in kind of a cloverleaf pattern. It's a timed event, and I had to admire the way Debra and Royal sailed around skimming the barrels.

When she told me what the horse cost, I blew up. Then she added a little fuel to the fire, "And I guess you'll really be mad when I tell you who's been teaching me to ride!"

I knew who it was, so I lied. "I don't care who gives you riding lessons, Debra."

"Oh?" Debra had a way of saying, "Oh" that meant a lot. In this case, it meant *You don't care if I've been spending a lot of time with the most attractive boy in the whole school?*

"I don't care, Debra," I lied again. For a minute I was worried, since a lie is bad news. It'll always catch up with you. And besides it's against the Bible.

She stared at me, then got red and finally said, "Well, that's just *fine*, Barney! I was afraid you were going to be *jealous!* But I can see you're above all that!"

She stomped off and I slunk off. What else can you do when you've made a first-class turkey of yourself?

Well, we made up the next day, mostly by sort of ignoring the whole thing. I knew that Jack was coming over to give her riding lessons pretty often. And he always managed to get one in when there was a crowd around. Sometimes he tried to egg me on to live it up. "Barney, that Debra girl sure did show me some riding yesterday. You ought to get with it yourself! Ever think about doing a little bronc ridin'?"

"Guess I don't want what few brains I've got kicked out, Jack!" I'd say.

"Well, it *do* take a real he-man to crawl on one of them critters!" He'd shrug, and I knew he was aiming it right at me. "Guess you know better than me what you can do."

So that was it. I was a lily-livered coward if I didn't get on one of those bucking horses. A test. Nobody stopped to think that if you put Jack into the door of a plane and asked him to parachute down, he might find it difficult. There were lots of things he'd probably feel pretty queasy about. For me, it was horses, but some people never think.

All through March and April I put up with it. If it hadn't been for Tim, my black-and-tan hound, I'd have been sunk, I guess. We went after coon and possum or even nothing at all, just to be in the woods. But every Monday morning I had to go back to school and put up with Jack Monroe. He was older than I was, a senior, and if I hadn't smarted off to him when he first came, I expect he'd have been too busy to notice me. But somehow, he wasn't the forgetting type, and I heard how he'd spread the word that Barney Buck was going to pay up for his smart mouth sooner or later.

Debra kept on practicing with Royal and went to a couple of high school rodeos. She didn't win, but she was getting better. I hadn't been able to go and see her until nearly the end of April, and then she just about made me agree to take her to the High School Rodeo in Benton.

I got through with all my chores at home and went to her house just in time to go. She had one of her dad's pickups, a neat Silverado with everything but a private bath loaded on it, and behind was a fancy horse trailer her dad had bought her. I wondered what it would be like to be so rich that you could buy your daughter a five-thousand-dollar toy and never even miss the money.

I was late, but we got there in plenty of

time. The Saline County Fairgrounds in Benton were right on Interstate 40. We pulled off and got Royal unloaded in time for Debra to saddle him up and ride him around the arena before the first event. I paid three dollars for a ticket and found myself a seat in the stands. Although we still had nearly an hour before rodeo time, quite a few people were already there. Most of them looked like couples who had kids entered. I got a sack of popcorn and a big Coke while the contestants rode their horses around to warm them up.

There were chutes at both ends of the arena. The west end held the calves for the roping events and the goats for the tying events.

I'd never been to a rodeo; so I kept watching the east end where I could see the humps of the bulls and the bucking horses. There were six chutes, and I was surprised to see that they were broadside to the arena. I mean, the horse in the chute wasn't *facing* out—he was sideways. When the gate opened, the horses and the bulls came out sideways.

I'd seen a few movies and TV shows about rodeos, but this was different. Besides the smell of animals and the sound of bulls bellowing, people were hollering at the animals. There was an air that you didn't get on TV!

After the kids had finally finished getting their horses warmed up, the announcer

15

blared out, "And now—it's rodeo time!"

First, there was the selection of rodeo queen. Young girls all dressed in sequins and fancy riding clothes rode around the arena, then lined up in front of the judges' stand. All of the girls got a flower in a vase. There were the third runner-up, the second, the first, and then the Rodeo Queen! It was like the Miss America Pageant, except that these girls were on horses.

After they got out of the way, the events started. I was pretty bug-eyed, the way you are with something new. First, there was the calf-roping event. A calf was released and a cowboy on his horse let him get about fifteen feet away, then took off after him, swinging his rope. The idea was to drop the rope over the calf's head, stop the horse, and jump off. Then when the calf jerked the end of the rope, the contestant had to run and throw the calf down, tie his legs with a short rope, and throw his hands up. Some of the cowboys missed catching the calf, but some of them did quite well, I thought.

Next was barrel-racing, which interested me the most. A girl on a horse came out of the west end of the arena, rode toward a set of barrels in a triangular position, then passed through an electric eye, which started her time. Most of the girls knocked over a barrel, and that added five seconds to their time, making it hard to win.

Soon it was Debra's turn. I was leaning

forward as she raced around the barrels.
Royal brushed one of them and it teetered.
Fortunately it steadied itself without falling,
and I gave a sigh of relief. Debra went
around the first two, then shot her horse
toward the single barrel at the other end of
the arena. She rounded it and drove Royal
into a hard, driving gallop toward the
starting point. When I heard the time, I
cheered along with the others. It was twenty-
one seconds—the best time so far. She won,
because the other girls either had knocked a
barrel over or had been too slow.

Debra came to sit beside me for the rest of
the show, and we watched the goat-tying. In
this event a girl rode her horse to the far end
of the arena, jumped off, threw the goat to
the ground, and tied his feet the way the
calf-ropers did. It was a timed event, and
Debra whispered, "I'm going to enter that
when we go to Prescott!"

Finally, there was the bareback riding. Was
it mean! The horses had one band around
their hind-quarters—just to make them buck,
Debra said—and one behind their front legs.
A little leather rig was tied at the base of the
horse's shoulder. Each rider wore gloves that
he worked into that rig. "If they fall off on
the left," Debra whispered in excitement,
"that's trouble! They can't get their hands out.
But if they fall off on the right side, why it's
all right."

The first horse named Gunshot came out so

fast that the boy on his back never got out of the chute. The horse gave a little twist, and the next thing the boy was in the dirt, scrambling to get up. "No ride for that cowboy!" the announcer bellowed out. "Now out of chute number two—Jack Monroe riding Magnum!"

A cowboy pulled the gate open, and I have to say Jack did what he was supposed to do. He raised his boots just as the horse's head went up, then let them fall back, and the horse hit with his front feet.

"Look at that rhythm!" Debra shouted. "He's spurring him just right!"

I didn't know anything about it, but I could see that Jack was just a part of the horse for those eight seconds. The horse spun and reared, but he was swinging his hand back and forth in perfect balance. I found out later that if the rider's free hand touches the horse, he's disqualified. I found out, too, that all the cowboys want the mean horses, because the judges score fifty points for the horse and fifty for the rider. So, with a poor mount there's no chance of winning.

Jack won that night. He stayed on for eight seconds. When the buzzer sounded, the two pickup men—cowboys who help the riders dismount—came to help, Jack took off his Stetson, gave a loud scream, and sailed his hat high into the air.

"Let's go down and congratulate him!" Debra said. I followed her down, and it seemed strange to be up on the platform where the cowboys got onto the bucking stock. The big bulls were being loaded into the chutes. We found Jack looking at a big red bull with horns unlike any I'd ever seen.

"Congratulations, Jack!" Debra said.

He looked up and saw her—and then me. "Well, thanks, Deb. And you brought Barney with you, I see."

"You sure did good, Jack," I said, trying to ignore his last comment. I was trying not to look at the bull, because a very strange thing had suddenly happened to me.

I'd always been a little frightened of high places and snakes. That bull—well, it just turned my legs to putty as I thought of what those horns could do to a guy!

I guess Jack saw me looking a little pale, because he grinned and said, "Hey, Buck, I heard one of the bull riders cancelled. I think I can get you on in his place. How about it?"

If he'd asked me to jump into a pit filled with rattlers, I would have felt about the same. When I managed to look at the bull, a Brahman with that big hump right behind his head, he swung his head, striking the wood of the chute with a loud *thunk*. That made me wonder what it would sound like if one of those horns hit my middle instead of the chute!

"I guess I'll pass," I said weakly.

Jack grinned at me and shot a quick glance at Debra. "You know, I *thought* you wouldn't be interested. Takes a real he-cat to ride the bulls!"

Then he lowered himself onto the bull, and we left, Debra leading the way. The gate came open, and I felt almost too sick to watch it. Jack stayed on for the full eight seconds; then he fell off and the bull turned right around and went for him! No matter how much I disliked Jack, I didn't want to see him get caught by one of those monsters!

Just then a clown came sailing out to take the bull's attention away from Jack, who managed to scramble up and get over the high bars of the arena.

Debra didn't say much as the rest of the bull riders went on, but I knew she was disappointed in me. Finally I had to say, "Look, Debra, I don't know anything about horses and bulls. It must take a lot of practice to learn how to ride those animals."

She was quiet a long time. Then she turned and faced me, a serious light glimmering in her dark eyes. "Barney, if *you* liked something real well—I mean *real* well—I'd get into it, because I like you."

I thought about that, then said, "Are you telling me I ought to get into rodeo because you're into it, Debra?"

"Yes, that's what I'm saying."

I thought about that some more, as we were loading Royal and were finally back into the truck. We were just about to Friendship before I had an answer for her.

"All right, Debra, if you think it ought to be that way, I'll–I'll think about it."

She suddenly slid over and gave me such a hard squeeze on the arm I nearly went off the road. "Oh, Barney! You *are* special sometimes!"

"Now watch out, Debra!" I said. "You want me to go off the road?"

"You're so *stodgie* most of the time, but when you just up and do something like this, Barney, I know I've got me a winner!"

TWO
Angel Unawares

We were just past the town of Friendship, and I had explained how I might get on a bucking horse, but would *never* get on one of those bulls. Debra gave me one of those looks that turned my thinking process into jelly. Then she said, "Look, Barney!"

I turned to my right and caught a glimpse of a man slumped against a tree. "Hey, that guy's face is covered! It looks pretty bad. Better see what's wrong."

"We're only going a few more miles," she said crossly. "Besides, he may be a criminal or something."

"Yeah, but Coach says we ought to help people like this guy." Without giving her time to argue, I slowed down and drove back to where the man was, then parked the truck along the shoulder and got out. Debra followed behind me.

"Hey, you all right?" I called. The man didn't move. "You better get out of this night air, mister."

He still didn't move. "Is he drunk, Barney?" Debra asked, peering cautiously at him, then at the old beat-up suitcase next to him.

"I don't know." I gave his shoulder a little shake, and he felt thin and almost boneless. The poncho that had covered his face fell down, showing his face. He looked around fifty and hadn't washed or shaved in quite a while.

"Is he dead?" Debra breathed nervously.

"I don't think so. It looks like he just passed out. We better get him into the truck and to a doctor fast."

We managed to get him to his feet, and he began mumbling weakly, "Lemme alone! Be all right!" Somehow we got him to the truck and onto the seat. I went back and got his suitcase and threw it in the back of the truck. Right away I got in and headed for the doctor.

"Barney, maybe we shouldn't be doing this," Debra said. "I mean, what if he dies!"

"You want to leave him on the highway?"

"Well, of course not! But we're never going to get a doctor tonight, Barney. They're all gone to the medical convention, except for Doctor James."

"Hey, I forgot about that. I wouldn't let that quack work on my dog! Look, I'll take him home with me tonight, and the first thing in the morning we'll take him to the hospital at Gurdon." I headed toward Debra's home.

"I'll see that Daddy pays for it," she said.

"Nope." I sounded a little short, but I was sensitive about her dad picking up the tab for something like this. Stingy as he was, I doubted that he'd pay it anyway!

"Well, if that's what you want to do. You call tomorrow and be careful. You don't know anything about him. Remember, he could be a criminal!"

"Could be an angel, too," I said, pulling into her driveway. "We have entertained angels unawares, the Bible says."

Debra looked at the old man propped up against the side of the cab, his mouth open. Most of his teeth were missing, and his cheeks were all sucked in. His hair was thick and white, but stiff with dirt and grime. He had the most weather-beaten face I'd ever seen. Wrinkles crisscrossed his cheeks, and his eyes were shut up like he'd been in the sun all his life. His hands were sort of gnarled and twisted, and he was lean as a wild boar hog in winter.

Debra shook her head. "I don't think he's an angel, Barney. Looks more like he just got out of the drunk tank at Hot Springs."

I stopped the truck in front of her house and Debra jumped out, saying, "Be careful!"

"I will." She waved good-bye, and I started for home—in the heart of Goober Holler, which was just as wild as it sounded. Our house was way off the highway, and when I got there, only the porch light was on. Joe and Jake, my brothers, were already in bed. Jake was snoring like a sawmill as usual.

The man was awake by now; so I was able to get him out of the truck and up to my room, but not without a real struggle. He was fighting mad and kept cussing and trying to resist me, but he was too weak. I guessed he had a fever; so I insisted he swallow a couple of aspirin before getting him to bed.

After I got him settled, I laid down on the nearby folding cot we kept for company and tried to read a chapter from the Bible. I'd promised Coach I would, but our overnight guest was cussing so much the reading didn't seem to be doing me much good.

If our visitor were an angel, he'd have to have been one of the fallen kind!

The next morning when Jake came to get me out of bed, he didn't notice me on the cot, but ran over and pulled the covers off the old man. Jake always did that to me; it was his idea of fun. This time he got the shock of his life!

I saw something rise up from my bed and wrap itself around Jake, and there was one of the most bloodcurdling screams I ever heard! The old man must have been scared out of his wits, waking up in a strange place with somebody ripping the covers off without warning. I jumped off the cot and tried to separate the two, who were rolling on the floor all wrapped up in a quilt. Both of them were hollering at the top of their lungs and flailing away with all they had.

"Jake!" I screamed. "Stop it, will you?"

"It's a killer, Barney!" Jake screamed back. "Hit him with something!"

The old man pulled loose from me and caught Jake with a feeble right hand, then collapsed with a gurgle.

"Now, you see what you've done?" I said. "Help me get him back in the bed."

"Who is that old man?" Jake demanded. "What's he doing in your bed?"

"I found him on the highway last night on the way home from the rodeo. He's real sick. I thought I'd take him to a doctor, but I guess maybe we better call Chief Tanner."

After we got the man back on the bed, we went downstairs and I called Chief. "You better stay there, Barney," he said. "I'll get Doc James and we'll see what to do."

Mrs. Simpkins, the lady who kept house for us, had a huge breakfast on the table. I dug into the hotcakes, sausages, grits, eggs, biscuits, and jelly and tried to explain the sick man upstairs at the same time.

Mrs. Simpkins loved anything tragic. She could see doom in a cookbook! I mean, her favorite part of the newspaper was the obituary page! She hadn't missed a funeral in years, and she had every disease described in *Reader's Digest*. She was a sweet woman, but she could describe a gory highway accident with as much pure enjoyment as most women talk about weddings.

She listened to my story, then nodded. "Probably an escaped lunatic. I'd be surprised if any of us woke up alive tomorrow morning."

"He's too sick," I said, spearing another hotcake.

"That kind is never too weak to do us dirty." She nodded with grim satisfaction and turned to Joe. "I want you to go see that new doctor who's just moved to town. Maybelle Simmons says he's *real* good. I'll bet he'll have you readin' and writin' in no time!"

Joe's problem was dyslexia, meaning he had a hard time reading. It wasn't a matter of being dumb, because Joe is smarter than Jake and I put together even if he is the youngest. But Mrs. Simpkins couldn't get it through her head that it wasn't something like the flu. She had the fixed idea that if Joe just got the right pill or saw the right doctor, he'd be able to read.

Joe smiled at her and said, "All right, Mrs. Simpkins." He looked just like our mom—same fair hair, clear skin, and the bluest eyes you ever saw.

Jake looked like our dad—short, muscular, and pretty much like an Indian. I don't know *whom* I looked like. Dad used to look at me—hair red as a dumb fire engine, tall as a stork, and freckles by the million. Then he'd say, "We found you under a mulberry bush!"

But when he'd rough me up and tousle my hair, I didn't mind his comment.

After our folks were killed in a car wreck, the State was going to put the three of us brothers in separate foster homes, but we'd managed to get the court's permission to come to Goober Holler, Arkansas, to my dad's old homeplace.

The one good thing was that Miss Jean Fletcher, the lady the court appointed to look out for us, was going to marry Coach Dale Littlejohn. They were going to live right here in town and adopt the three of us. Miss Jean was still finishing up a degree at a university; so we were on hold until then.

Anyway, about nine o'clock Chief Tanner pulled into the yard and got out of his police car. He was around fifty and in good shape. There were some pretty rough people in Clark County, but as far as I knew, none of them had ever given Chief Tanner any problems.

"Well, I brought the doc, Barney," he said.

I turned just as Doctor James was getting out of the car. He was a small man with a big head. He looked as if he'd just bitten into a sour pickle. He'd been put on probation two or three times by the medical board for something or other. "All right, all right!" he grunted. "Let's get this done."

Chief Tanner glared at him. "Just an example of the loving country doctor, ain't you, Ed?"

"He's in my room upstairs to the right, Doctor," I said, pointing to the second floor. Doctor James went in, and I told Chief about how I'd found our guest.

"I reckon I'll be able to find out if he's wanted," Chief finally commented.

"I don't think he's a criminal. Just looked sick to me."

Doctor James didn't waste much time. He came out with his little black bag and said, "One of these fancy new viruses. Get this prescription filled and keep him in bed for a few days—and feed him while you're at it."

I stared at him. "But shouldn't he be in the hospital?"

"You gonna pay for it?" he snapped. "Do what you please. I've done my Christian duty. Do too much of this charity work as it is! Let's go, Chief."

Chief Tanner stared at him, then shook his head and sighed. He looked at me and said, "Barney, I reckon I can put him up—except my wife is ailing herself. But if you . . ."

"Oh, shoot, Chief, I guess we can tend him for a few days. Give Mrs. Simpkins a little practice."

"Well, I hate to do it, but if you can handle it, I think it'll be best. I'll check with you later on, Ed."

So, that was the way it started, and at first it was fairly simple. We found out our guest's name was Jim Bob Puckett, and he didn't have any relatives we could contact as far as we could tell. He slept most of the time, waking up just to eat and go to the bathroom.

On the third day, he woke up and stared at me across the room. "Where in tarnation is this place?" he said in a high-pitched voice. "Well, can you talk?" That triggered a coughing fit.

I got him a glass of water and began explaining some things while he drank.

"I'm Barney Buck, and this is my house," I said matter-of-factly. "I found you sick on the freeway three days ago. We got a doctor and have been taking care of you."

"Well, who asked you to?" he said, glaring at me out of his faded blue eyes. "I don't recollect *sendin'* for you."

I stared at him. "Well, of all the ungrateful. . . ."

"Gimme my britches!" he said, throwing back the covers. He stood up and bent over to pick up his shirt, which was hanging on the back of a chair near the bed. Then he fell flat on the floor.

I picked him up and couldn't resist saying, "I hope you don't mind if I help you back into bed?"

Then I was sorry. He was so light! I was pretty big and fairly strong for my age, but even though he was a full-grown man, he was easier to pick up than Joe! And when he fell back on the pillow, I took one look at his face and felt real bad about having been sharp with him. He looked worn out, and I wondered what it felt like to be old and sick with nobody but strangers to take care of you.

That was when I made up my mind that whatever it took to get Jim Bob Puckett up and going, I was going to get the job done. Maybe if I'd known how cantankerous the old buzzard was going to be, I wouldn't have made that decision!

THREE
The Goober
Burger

"Jim Bob, I can put up with your snoring.
Maybe I'll get used to your lazy, trifling ways
if you stay around long enough. But if you
don't stop leaving those nasty spit cups all
over the house, I'm going to shoot you!"

I glared at Jim Bob, who was sitting on a
cane-bottomed chair on the front porch. He'd
been with us two weeks and had gotten over
his virus. He'd also found a home! Where else
could he sit on a nice, shady front porch all
day long, chew tobacco to his heart's content,
get three squares a day, and live like a king?

"Well, now, boy, I'll tell ya the truth," he
said evenly. "I could give up eatin' a heap
easier than I could give up my dippin'."

"Yeah? Well, it doesn't look to me like
you've given up anything—except work!"

"Why, boy, I been sick! You wouldn't make a

sick man get hisself a backset, would you now? Why, even a no-count *Yankee* wouldn't hardly do a trick like that!"

It drove me crazy! As soon as he was able to get out of bed, I thought he'd be moving on, but he just settled in like some long-lost relative. I hinted around a couple of times that he try to find a place to stay, but he never took the hint.

"Why, shucks, boy, this here place is just *fine*," Jim Bob would say appreciatively. Then he'd settle back on his chair and with a razor-sharp knife make a pile of thin cedar shavings from a block of wood and anoint the porch with Skoal.

I tried to get Chief to do something, but he wouldn't do anything. "You can chuck him out anytime you want, Barney," he said. "Don't need no law for that." Then he gave me one of his grins. "Reckon your Christian charity is gettin' tested a bit, ain't it, son?"

Coach Littlejohn told me about the same thing. "What do you think Jesus would have done in a case like this?"

There's never been any easy answer to that; so I just made up my mind to put up with the old fellow the best I could.

Actually, he was two men—a grumpy, griping, mean old cuss most of the time and when he wanted to, a real nice guy. Joe thought he was just great, and the two spent lots of time together. I was glad of that, but it worried me when I noticed that Jake and Jim

Bob were getting thick as thieves. They'd gotten into the habit of going off to Jake's room, and I was afraid they were cooking up some wild scheme.

It was a sure bet they were, considering that my brother Jake was the greatest con artist to hit the western world since PT Barnum!

Just to give you an idea of what he could do, last spring he put on a drive to sell edible pets—BUCK'S EDIBLE PETS. He got people all over the county to buy animals that are cute when they're small: chickens, ducks, goats, pigs, rabbits. The idea was that the kids could play with the things when they were small and then when the animals got big, they could be eaten.

Like most of Jake's wild schemes, it sounded pretty good at first, but it backfired. What happened was that lots of people bought the cute little things, but when it came time to eat them, the kids had gotten so attached to them, it was a tragedy to even talk about eating them! The upshot was that we had to give most of the money back, and to this day some people in town won't even speak to me. Somehow they figured it was *my* fault, not Jake's.

Looking back on it, I think what triggered the whole mess they got me into was the visit Jim Bob and I made over to the Crockett place. I was a partner of sorts with Judd Crockett in the Charger, a stock car he raced.

His sister Dandy was in most of my classes. That's why we saw each other a lot.

My old pickup wasn't running right; so I ran over to get Judd to smooth it out. Jim Bob got up from his seat on the porch, stretched, and sighed. "Guess I'll go with you, boy. I'm getting' a bit tired of this place."

"Yeah, it's a shame how whittling and spitting tobacco juice wears a body out, Jim Bob!"

He grinned at me, then said, "I'm about over my sick spell, boy. Then you'll see some *real* work from a Texas man."

We went to the Crockett place and found Judd working on the Charger near a big sycamore tree and Dandy was helping him. I noticed a young girl sitting on a washtub nearby.

"Hi, Barney." Judd grinned. "That thing sounds like a washing machine," he said, waving a socket toward the truck.

"That's why I brought it for you to fix," I said. "Hello, Dandy."

"Hi, Barney," Dandy said. She was a pretty girl with dark brown hair and the clearest skin I ever saw except for a few freckles, which (unlike mine) made her look better. "This is my cousin, Tater Crockett."

She went into a long story of whose brother's second cousin had married a third half-aunt and got me lost as usual. The Crocketts had more members in their family than the Democratic Party, and from time to

35

time one of them would surface at their place. It never surprised me to meet a stranger there, because they had some sort of signals like ants, I guess, to get the family together.

"Hi, Tater," I said. It sounded like a funny name for a girl, but two of Dandy's sisters are named Petunia and Hydrangea; so I never got too surprised over the names of the Crockett girls. "You here for a visit?"

She gave me a funny look, then said, "N–no. I'm living here now."

Judd gave me a shake of his head, then said, "Tater comes from Texas."

"Texas!" Jim Bob had finally gotten out of the truck and ambled over to where we were standing. He grinned at Tater and stuck his gnarled hand out. "Shake hands with a Texas man, honey! I bet I would of knowed a pretty, little thing like you was from Texas without bein' told!"

Tater gave him a quick look, then smiled for the first time and shook hands with him. "Are you *really* from Texas?" she asked.

"Sure as my name's Jim Bob Puckett! But, honey, you ought not to ask a man is he from Texas."

"Why not?"

" 'Cause if he *is*, he'll tell you without bein' asked! And if he *ain't*—why, shoot, there ain't no need in shamin' him!"

Judd laughed and said, "You're from Texas, all right. Staying at the Bucks', are you?"

"Jest till I get my strength back."

Judd looked at him and said, "I wonder if you know anything about horses—being a Texas man?"

Jim Bob narrowed his eyes and said dryly, "Well, I reckon I know one end from another."

"Tater here has found a horse she likes," Judd said. "Belongs to old man Dillard. Now I don't know anything about horses and don't want to. She's been pestering me to go over and take a look at the thing. What say you go do that while I fix the truck? Here's the keys." Judd then threw Jim Bob his keys.

"Come along with a gentleman," Jim Bob said with a grin. Dandy, Tater, and Jim Bob piled into the old Ford that Judd drove to work and went out of the yard in a cloud of dust.

I watched them and said, "I hope he can ride a horse better than he can drive a car."

"Can't hurt that wreck much," Judd said grinning. "I wouldn't ask Tater about her home, if I was you. Her daddy went off when she was just a baby, and then just two months ago her mama died. She doesn't have anywhere to go; we just took her in. And you know, the real sad thing is about her horse."

"Her horse?" I asked.

"Kid is crazy about horses," Judd said. "Seems like when her mom died, they sold everything—including the kid's horse. That's been what she's missed most, except for her mom. That's why I was sort of hoping we could get this horse from Dillard. But you know how tight he is!"

It got to me, maybe because I'd lost my own folks. "Gee, I hope you can get it, Judd."

"Well, we just about scrape by now. It would have to be real cheap, and then there's feed and all."

"Yeah, I heard *that!*" I said with a nod. "But it would sure be good if she had something of her own."

Judd got the car fixed in about thirty minutes, and we sat around and talked about cars until Jim Bob and the girls got back. When Tater got out of the car, I could see her face glowing.

"Judd, Jim Bob says he's a great horse! Can we get him? Can we?"

"Wait a minute now, Tater," Judd said. "We have to do a lot of thinking about this. Jim Bob, what did you think—and how much?"

Jim Bob hobbled up to the porch for a glass of lemonade that Dandy had just held up to him. He let the stuff trickle down his throat before answering. "Well, to tell the truth, I was plain flabbergasted. I was kinda expectin' a beat-up old nag but it was one of the best-lookin' quarterhorses I seen in a long time. I tried him out, and let me say, folks, he is a jim-dandy!"

"You rode him?" I asked in surprise. His arthritis probably hadn't been so bad, or it would've kept him from getting on a horse.

"Did he ever!" Tater shouted. "And he says he can be a *great* horse to run barrels on!"

"Wait a minute," Judd said. "How much is he?"

"Why, I reckon Dillard don't know what he's got." Jim Bob grinned. "He only wants a thousand for the animal."

"A thousand dollars!" Judd groaned. "Might as well be a million!"

"Son, that ain't no money for a horse like that. Course, he ain't registered, but he's got the stuff. Train him right, and you could get six, maybe seven, thousand for him anyday."

"Yeah, but we don't have even *one* thousand now!" Judd said. He looked down at Tater and said, "We'll find you a horse, all right, but not this one."

All the light went out of her face, and she turned her head away, tears starting. She didn't whine, but said in a muffled voice, "Sure, Judd. I understand." Then she walked away, looking down at the ground.

As soon as she was in the house, Judd kicked a pillar of the porch and said, "I feel like I just drowned a puppy!"

"Isn't there *some* way, Judd?" Dandy pleaded. "She's so alone!"

Judd studied a button on his shirt for a long time, then looked at me and said, "Well, Barney, I guess you're going to have to get busy with your prayer line—like you did for me!"

He smiled when he said it, but I knew that

he really appreciated the time we Bucks stood by him when he was in trouble. I'd told him then that God answers prayers, and he had just laughed. The way it worked out, though, he just about *had* to believe it. Now he nodded and said, "You get to praying, and I'll try to win a big race so we can get that horse for Tater."

We left soon after that, and Jim Bob didn't say a word all the way home. I knew he was thinking about Tater and that horse. "Jim Bob, it's a shame that girl can't get that horse. Is he really that good?"

He nodded and said, "He's got what it takes, boy. And that little gal from Texas is gonna have him!"

He spoke so loudly that I was surprised. "Well, it would take a miracle. . . ."

"Don't gimme none of your preachin', boy! I got enough of that when I was growin' up!"

"But how else . . . ?"

"Boy, I'm a Texas man! And if a Texas man says he'll do something, it'll get done. You hear me?"

When we got home, he went right into the house looking for Jake. They holed up in Jake's room for the rest of the day, and I knew that trouble was ahead. Jake's schemes always spelled trouble, and with Jim Bob to egg him on, there was no limit on what they could get me into!

I found out what it was a week later.

Coach asked me to go to Lake Nixon just outside of Little Rock to be a counselor for the younger boys in our church, and I had so much fun there I just forgot about Jake and Jim Bob. But I thought of it when Coach and I dropped all the kids off at church, and he was driving me home.

"That sure was a good time for the boys, Coach, and for me, too."

"And for me, too, Barney." Coach smiled at me, then dropped his arm around my shoulder, which always made me feel funny. I mean, when he and Miss Jean got married, he'd be my *real* dad, and that would be strange to me. Why, if I'd hunted the world over, I could never have found one man who would suit me better, and Jake and Joe felt the same. He'd been a pro football player, and he still looked like one. Besides, he liked to hunt and fish, and he was the best Sunday school teacher in the universe!

He started to say something else, then suddenly his jaw dropped. "What in the world . . . ?" he gasped, pointing toward a stand on the highway in front of us.

I took one look and then covered my face. "Oh, no! They've done it!"

The large hand-painted sign said: BUCK'S GOOBER BURGERS. Under that it said in dripping red paint: ALL YOU CAN EAT—TWO DOLLARS!

"Why, you can't buy burger meat for less

than a dollar and a half a pound! They'll get us arrested for poverty or something!" I groaned.

"No law against being poor," Coach said. "Knowing Jake, he may have an angle on this thing."

"He only wants to drive me crazy!" I said as we pulled up and got out of the car.

Five other cars were pulled up in the large area the highway department had used to dump gravel on a long time back. It made a perfect spot for a drive-in. I recognized the big trailer we'd used on another of Jake's schemes—a dog wash. Now on top of it was a cabin of sorts built out of plywood, with a big counter right in front. There was Jake handing out burgers and Cokes in paper cups, a huge smile covering his face.

"That'll be four dollars, please," he said and whipped the money into a cigar box on the counter. Then he saw Coach and me and hollered, "Hey, Barney and Coach, welcome to the Goober Bar! What'll it be? On the house!"

I sputtered at him, I was so angry. "Jake, you've flipped! You can't sell hamburgers at this price."

"These ain't hamburgers," he said calmly. "They're Goober Burgers right from the heart of Goober Holler! Try one."

"Guess we better," Coach said, and we both took the sandwiches that Jake pulled out of a little bun warmer. I took the wrapper off and sniffed it. "Well, they *smell* good," I said.

"And they *taste* good!" Coach said in surprise. "A little hot—but great!"

I bit into mine, and sure enough, it was pretty good. A sort of cross between barbecue and hamburger. The meat was ground up fine, and there was a lot of hot sauce in it, but it was better than anything we could get at the local hamburger joint.

"What's in it?" I asked, taking another bite.

Jake shook his head and said, "Sorry, Barney. That's a professional secret. My partner says it's an old Indian recipe he learned from the Apaches in Texas."

"Jim Bob is your partner?" I asked.

"Sure! He furnishes the grub and I do the serving," Jake said.

"Who does the cooking?" Coach asked.

"Oh, he does the meat, and I do the rest," Jake replied.

"What is the *rest?*" I asked. "Looks like the Goober Burger is all you serve."

"Well, we have potato chips and Zero bars," Jake said.

"You making any money?" Coach asked.

"Now, Coach, that's kind of a personal question! Do I ask if *you're* making any money?"

"Where's Jim Bob?" I asked, knowing that Jake would never talk about money if he could help it.

"Gone to get more supplies. We're running low."

Coach and I sat there for over an hour and

counted at least twenty cars that stopped. It was in a good place, because there wasn't another place to eat for twenty miles on each stretch. Everybody bought a lot of chips, Cokes, and candy, too; so it looked like a success—Jake was cleaning up.

Finally, Jim Bob came up driving *my* truck and nodded to us. "Howdy, boy. Help me get this here meat inside, will you?"

He had a bunch of chopped meat in about five big pans, and it smelled good. I helped him get them up to Jake, who started making burgers like mad. "We gotta have more Cokes, Jim Bob, and lots more kinds of candy—and get some peanuts, too."

Well, they just got after it, those two, and for a week they sold more grub than they could get ready. "What'll you do with all the money you're making, Jim Bob?" I asked once.

He gave me a straight look. "I told you about Texas men, boy. That little girl is gonna have that horse!"

"Gee, I think that's great!" I said.

Then he had to add, "And there ain't no *prayin'* necessary, boy! I'll take care of this my own self!"

Well, it looked as if he might do it. I never knew what they were making, but Jim Bob scurried around like a teenager. He never mentioned his arthritis. I let him use my truck and he was gone a lot. I figured out he was getting the meat from a wholesale butcher in Prescott or maybe even in Hot Springs, and I knew for sure they had a deal for day-old buns with all the local stores.

I saw Tater once, but she was bright as a bluetick puppy—smiling and falling all over herself, helping out at the Crocketts.

"I don't know about this business with Jim Bob and that horse," Judd said one day. "He don't look like he's got a thousand bucks to throw away. You think he's—well, do you reckon he's. . . ."

He couldn't say it, but I knew what he meant. Jim Bob was an old man and Tater was a young girl. "No chance of that, Judd," I said quickly. "He just wants to do it."

"Well, if you say so. She sure has been different since this came up."

All in all, I was happy. Jake was making money, and Jim Bob had found a way to make a living—at least for a while—and then, of course, Tater was going to get her horse.

Mrs. Simpkins didn't like it. "Mark my words, no good will come of it!" she said.

"We won't get *too* cheerful, not with you to keep us aware of all the disasters just around the corner," I said, then grinned at her.

"I know you think I'm too gloomy, but you'll see. I got a feeling!" She always did have a feeling that the worst would happen; so I paid no attention to her.

Maybe I should have, although it wouldn't have made any difference.

FOUR
The White Feather

"Another couple of weeks, Jim Bob says, and I can buy Don Pedro!"

Tater was helping out at the Goober Burger stand where I'd stopped off on the way to town to see if they needed any supplies. Jake was sitting out under a big bull pine tree, listening to Jim Bob tell some of his lies about how good things used to be, and they were letting Tater do all the work.

"Hey, that's *great*, Tater," I said. "Guess you'll be riding the barrels real soon."

She gave me a wide smile and answered, "Oh, Jim Bob says it'll be a few weeks, but I told Debra to expect some competition."

"Well, that'll be pretty hard on me, won't it?"

"What do you mean, Barney?"

"Why, I'll have my two best girls competing

against each other. How'll I know who to root for?"

"Oh, Barney, Debra's your girl!"

"Well, as I've tried to explain to Debra lots of times, kids our age ought not to get too *serious*. You know what I mean?"

"Sure I do."

"Well, shoot, I wish you'd explain it to Debra! She just can't understand how that is."

Tater patted me on the arm and gave me a big smile. "Maybe I can tell her so she'll understand, Barney. Sometimes it takes a girl to talk to a girl."

That night I told Jim Bob how swell it was for him to help Tater buy the horse.

"Well, I ain't never had no younguns of my own and I sure would like to see that Texas gal get that hoss," he said humbly.

"Looks good, doesn't it, Jim Bob? I mean with the Goober Burger stand doing so well."

"Ain't nothin' sure, boy, not in this world." He chewed his mustache and added, "But looks like this time I'm going to do 'er!"

"Don't count your chickens before they hatch!" Mrs. Simpkins was sitting across the room in a Boston rocker, knitting a pair of socks. She stared at us with a mouth like a purse and added, "There's many a slip 'twixt the cup and the lip."

Jim Bob stared at her, then said, "Well, I reckon if anybody ought to know about that, it's me, ma'am."

He got up and hobbled off to bed. I could

tell he felt pretty put down by her remarks. He didn't know Mrs. Simpkins wasn't nearly as gloomy as she talked.

"You sure did cheer him up!" I said and stalked off to bed, wondering if there was any way to have her lips glued up.

The next afternoon, the ax fell.

I was at the Buck's Burger Bar helping Joe and Tater handle the crowd, which was pretty big since a lot of vacationers were passing through.

"This your place of business?"

I looked up to see a tall woman with a long face like a horse staring at me. She had hard eyes about the color of spit and a mouth that looked like a number eleven bear trap. Her voice was loud, with a hard edge on it, and when I hesitated, she said, "Are you the proprietor of this stand, I asked."

"Well, not actually, ma'am."

"I am RD Simmons of the State Board of Health. I have had reports that you are selling food in this place that is in violation of the regulations of our department." She gave a sniff and looked around inside the stand. "If you will open the door, I will make my inspection."

I looked over at Joe and Tater, who had turned a little pale. The woman looked more like a wrestler than a food inspector. "Do you have any identification, ma'am?" I asked.

"Certainly!" She whipped out a card with

her picture on it. It was about as hard-looking as she was. But it was official, so I unhooked the door and she came in.

It didn't take her long to look, because we had only one grill and it was spotless. The meat was in an old icebox that Jake had liberated somewhere along with the cold drinks.

"I have to see the place where this meat is prepared," she snorted.

"Well, I don't know about that," I said. "My brother takes care of all the details."

"I know where it is," Joe said.

"You must show me or I'll have to get a warrant."

"Tater, can you mind the stand while I take this lady to where the stuff is fixed?"

"Sure, Barney, but. . . ."

"I insist that you close this place down until I have completed my inspection," the woman said with a sour look, "and give me one of those things. What do you call them?"

"Goober Burgers," Joe said. He handed her one, and she unwrapped it and took a bite. She chewed slowly, and I could tell she was trying to find something wrong with it, but she didn't say anything. Finally she ate the whole thing, then said, "Let's go. In case you're wondering, I take my job seriously. I always eat whatever is prepared at any place I inspect."

"I hope you liked it." Joe smiled.

"That's not important," she sniffed. "I'll not allow my personal preferences to affect my integrity."

"Well, I guess we better go. Joe, you want to show us where Jim Bob fixes the meat?"

We got in her car and she said, "You must not touch anything, you boys."

I didn't have any urge to touch her old car, and I just sat there as Joe directed her. He took us to the old Roberts place, which wasn't too far from our place. It had been abandoned a long time ago, but I saw that the smokehouse was still in use. A slow wreath of smoke was climbing out into the sky, and Joe said, "That's where Jim Bob smokes the meat."

We all got out, and Miss RD Simmons marched right in. It was dark, of course, but she checked pretty close. She tried to find someplace where flies could get in, but it was tight and screened. She tried to find bugs, but there weren't any. She looked for half an hour trying to find something wrong, but finally she sniffed and said, "I'll have to make a more thorough inspection later."

"That means everything is all right," I whispered to Joe, and he gave me a hug.

We were almost to the car when she asked, "Do you know where the meat is dressed? I have to check that."

"I don't know," I said.

"*I* do!" Joe said.

"Is the slaughterhouse too far?" she asked.

"I suppose it's in the country miles away."

"Oh, no, ma'am," Joe said quickly. "It's right over there." He pointed toward a thicket about fifty yards from the house.

"There?" Miss Simmons said with a sudden look in her eye that spelled *no good* for the Goober Burger Bar. "Show me."

Joe led the way, and we stepped inside a little open space inside the thicket. It was obvious that somebody had been butchering. The place was like the one I had for cleaning the coons Tim and I brought home. Miss Simmons took a wild look around and made a funny noise in her throat. "You mean to say that the meat you use at that place is slaughtered and dressed here?"

Joe shifted and gave a little nod.

"Well! We'll see about this!" She turned to go, saying, "I will have to see the beef that is used in this operation. It is substandard, too, no doubt."

"Oh, no, ma'am! It ain't substandard beef!" Joe said quickly.

"*You* would hardly be a qualified judge," she snorted, then turned to go back to the car.

The thing is, we came in by one little path, and the one we took going back was a different one. She was plowing through the bushes toward the yard when I heard her kick something and say, "What's that?"

I caught up with her and looked down to see what she'd kicked. What I saw made me just about jump out of my boots!

"Well, what is it?" she said impatiently. "Don't just stand there! Look, there's another one—and there's one. Why they're all over the place!"

"Yes, ma'am, they are," I said.

"But what in the world *are* they?" She leaned over and picked up a round object. It was sort of dusky dark in the woods so she brought it up close to her face to see. There was a long silence; then she screamed, "It's an armadillo! Oh, get it off me!"

She was hollering and running around in the woods trying to get away from the armadillo shell, but she stepped on another shell and went down with a crash right in the middle of a big pile of shells.

"Get me out!" she began screaming. "Oh, save me!"

"They're not alive, Miss Simmons," I told her. "They're just old shells."

Finally we got her up, which was like raising the Titanic, and she went running down the path until we finally got into the open.

She stopped and slowly turned around, a strange look on her horsey face. She stared at the thicket and whispered, "What are those shells?"

"That's what I was trying to tell you, Miss Simmons," Joe said. "We don't serve no substandard beef, 'cause Goober Burgers are made out of. . . ."

"Armadillo!" she screamed.

Her face turned a sort of lime green, and her eyes bulged out. Then suddenly she clapped her hand over her mouth, turned, and made a run for the car.

She never made it, though.

While Joe and I waited off a distance till she finished, Joe asked, "Do you think we'll pass the inspection, Barney?"

I looked at Miss RD Simmons and shook my head. "Joe, about the *best* thing that can happen to us is not to get sent to jail. But if she has anything to do with it, looks like Devil's Island would be about our best bet!" I looked over at Miss Simmons and said, "I guess she's about finished. Come on. I want to tell Mrs. Simpkins the bad news. She'll enjoy it almost as much as the last time they used the electric chair at Cummings!"

The end of Buck's Goober Burger Bar was somewhat like a pileup at the Indy 500.

The place was closed down, of course, by the Department of Health. There was a fine, too, which pretty well wiped out the profits that Jim Bob and Jake had made. The whole town got the word when there was a front-page story in our little daily paper, which I call *The Daily Mistake*. I had to take a lot of ribbing from all my friends, but, of course, the worst thing was that it knocked the props out from under Tater Crockett.

Jim Bob was hard hit, too. He sat on the

front porch whole days at a time, just staring out into space, and once or twice he went on a big binge in Hot Springs.

"It's not your fault, Jim Bob," I told him. "You did your best. John Wayne couldn't have done any better."

He glared at me and muttered, "When a Texas man don't come through on his word, it's got to be a sad state of affairs."

I guess it would have been pretty bad on me, but the truth is that I only felt bad for two days.

The bar closed down on Thursday, and on Saturday night I went to a rodeo in Fort Smith. It was a long drive and I was pretty tired, but Debra was anxious to enter the barrel riding; so I drove her up.

She took first place again. Judd had come along with Dandy, Tater, Petunia, and Hydrangea to cheer us on. I was surprised to see Jim Bob there with them, but he was.

Well, I drew a horse, and one of the guys next to me whistled under his breath and looked at me sort of funny. "Lots of luck, fella!"

"Bad horse?" I asked.

"Well, he ain't actually killed nobody—not *yet!*"

I swallowed hard and hung around waiting for my ride. When it was time, I found Jim Bob at the chute waiting to ease me onto the horse.

I got a real scare when the horse reared up

and I nearly fell off, but Jim Bob just held on and got the horse quieted down. When the chute opened, I was ready—scared, but ready.

I'd worked my right hand into the glove I'd practically soaked with rosin and then had locked into the rigging. It was so tight in there you'd think I was going to stay until Judgment Day. I knew that if I fell off, it had better be on the right side, since I'm right-handed. If I fell that way, my hand would slide free. But if I fell on the left side of the animal, my hand would stick and there was a real good chance of getting kicked in the head!

I heard the announcer say, "And here comes Barney Buck on Mankiller!" I guess there was lot of noise, but a funny thing happened.

As Mankiller shot free of the chute, it was as if I were in a big empty room without any noise, or at least I didn't hear any. I could smell the stench of the hay behind the chute. The lights overhead broke apart as I began pounding up and down, kind of like the sparklers you light on Christmas. I could hear the creaking of the rigging and the sound of Mankiller's hooves punching the ground and the grunting noises he made, but that was all.

My head was popping back and forth as the jolting hops of the horse threw my body back and forth like a limp dishrag, but suddenly it was easy!

I was doing all the right things: lifting my spurs to the horse's shoulders right in time with his jumps, throwing my arm back and forward to keep my balance, rolling on top of the horse in perfect time.

For a second we were no longer two separate things, but a blurred unity of flesh and blood!

I only had to stay on for eight seconds, but it was so easy I was surprised to hear the buzzer go off.

The pickup men were right there, and I just leaned over and caught the arm of one of them, and he set me down light as a feather.

Then the announcer said, "Now, folks, you ain't seen no ridin' like *that* in a spell, have you?" There was a roar of applause and I nodded my head. The announcer called out my score, which was almost perfect, and there was another roar from the crowd. The judges give fifty points for the horse and fifty points for the rider. If you get a listless horse, you're not going to win the money and that's all there is to it.

"And the score is 92! Let's hear it for Barney Buck, folks!"

I was met at the fence by a whole bunch of people, including Tater, who threw her arms around my neck right in front of everybody. Well, in front of Debra, who was standing off to one side looking a little strange. She didn't come over to me; so I went over to her and said, "Well, looks like we both had good nights, huh?"

"Tater tells me you're having a hard time explaining to me about how we're not going together." She stood stiffly with her arms at her sides and glared at me.

"What did you say?" I was still excited by the ride, and then I remembered what I'd said to Tater. "Oh, that! Well, I've tried to tell you, Debra, about how we're too young to go steady and all that. . . ."

"Yes, she *explained* all that. I'm sorry you find me so dense, Barney. But I think I understand you at last."

"Oh, Debra, don't be like that!" I tried to take her hand, but she pulled it back as if I were a snake or something. "That Tater is just real pathetic, Debra. You just don't know how much trouble she's had. I'm just trying to help her."

"Fine! You just fly right at it, Barnabas!"

When she called me *that*, I could see the sparks flying!

Maybe we would have gotten over it, but right then smiling Jack Monroe came over. He was smiling like usual, but not so big. I had beat him out of first place, and he didn't like it.

"Hey, great ride, Buck!" he said. He stuck his hand out and tried to crunch my bones the way he always did. "You did right well. Now if you'd just let me give you a few pointers, why I think you might get yourself a belt buckle like this one." He pointed at his silver belt buckle, which said ALL STATE CHAMPION.

"I think Barney did very well, Jack," Debra said at once. She might have been angry with me, but she wasn't about to let him ride over me like that.

"Well, sure, that's what I say." Then he got a little light in his eye. Most of the people from Cedarville were gathering around, and he raised his voice so that they could all hear. "You hear about Nick Tolliver? No? Well, his car broke down over by Pencil Bluff. So that means somebody can have his shot at the bull riding. How about it, Barney? You might get to be all-around cowboy if you can ride a bull."

"No!" Tater said suddenly. "Those bulls are too dangerous."

"Barney hasn't had any experience," Judd said. "I wouldn't get on one of those things for a million dollars!"

My mouth had turned to answer Jack's challenge, and I kept waiting for one voice—Debra's, telling me not to do it. But she didn't say a word.

"You want to see me try it, Debra?" I asked.

"Oh, you better not," she said. But I suddenly knew that she *did* want me to do it. For some reason or another.

Why do guys do dumb, dangerous things just because a girl wants them to? I guess if I knew the answer to that, I'd get rich quick!

"All right, I'll do it!" I said, before I realized what I'd said.

Everybody started telling me not to do it. Everybody except Debra, who kept looking at me.

Finally I said, "Jack, where do I sign up?"

"Already got your bull," he said. "Only one left; so you just come with me and we'll get you signed aboard that critter. Name is Terminal Disease." He grinned and said, "Got a bad name, but you just mind what I tell you and you probably won't get hurt too bad."

Well, I signed up feeling like I was signing my own death certificate. Then Jack started telling me all about what to do and what not to do. He had an extra rigging, and the first thing I knew, the bull riding had started.

"Got to leave you now and make my ride. But I'll be right back to help you get on this animal," he said.

After he left, I went into some kind of shock. I was right there beside the fifth chute where Terminal Disease was waiting. I moved up closer and stared at him through the slats in the chute. He was a brindle gray and weighed about two tons. He was not moving, but I saw that he was staring right at me, as if he knew who I was.

I forgot where I was, and my heart was racing like a machine gun. My mouth got so dry I couldn't even swallow, and my legs felt so weak I thought I might fall down.

Several rides went on, but I was locked in with that bull. We just stared at each other, and I felt more and more sick, the way you would with a bad case of the flu.

Then Jack came up and said, "Well, nobody's done too good, Buck. Maybe you can win. Get on this bull now."

I looked over at the stands, and I felt I had a zoom lens. I could see all the Crocketts and Debra and Jim Bob in their seats. And then I looked back at Terminal Disease. Jack was saying something to me, and I found myself crawling up on top of the chute. I stared down at the broad back of the bull, and he swung his head to one side so that the tips of his huge horns banged against the wood. Then he gave a deep grunt.

"Ease on, Buck," Jack said, and I actually raised one leg and got ready to rope on. I tried to tell myself it was just a big horse. I hadn't been afraid of the bucking stock, but then it happened.

Terminal Disease suddenly reared up, and I caught a glimpse of the whites of his eyes. He bawled at me so loud that it raised the hair on the back of my neck!

I don't really remember getting down from the chute. I must have because I found myself running into the darkness, into the big field behind the chutes, running as if a demon from the pit were after me. I was sobbing, too. I ran until I got to a line of trees, then ran some more until all the sounds of the rodeo faded and all the lights from the stands were cut out by the trees and the clouds.

Finally I couldn't run any more; I fell against a big tree and lay there.

The only thing I wanted was to stay there in the dark forever.

Everyone in that place had seen me show a yellow streak—a white feather. It was the coldest, longest night of my life, and I wished that I could die there in the dark instead of going back to face those people.

In the end I got up and went back to the lights and the noise, but I wasn't the same guy who'd come to that rodeo.

FIVE
The Pity Party

Uncle Dave Simmons, Debra's grandfather, heard about a man who got angry at the pastor's sermon on lust. Uncle Dave said, "If you throw a rock at a whole pack of dogs, the only one who'll holler is the one who gets hit!"

For about a week after I turned tail and ran at the rodeo, I was like that. Every time I heard someone say something about being scared, I was ready to fight him.

I was waiting to fill my gas tank at the Exxon station and heard Mitch Conroy say to Tom Gambrell, ". . . Was jest plain scared to death, he was!"

I slammed the nozzle into the tank and shoved my face right up close to Mitch's. "You know a lot about it, don't you now? Maybe if you got a little closer to an animal like that, you wouldn't be so quick to judge other people!"

Mitch's mouth dropped open, and he and Tom stared at each other, then back at me. Finally Tom said, "Gee, Barney, Mitch was just telling me about the time his Uncle Fred got in a fire fight over in Vietnam in the war."

"Yeah, Barney, I wasn't making fun of Fred! Why, he's got a silver star and all kinds of medals."

I turned red, then mumbled something about being sorry, but they gave me funny looks from then on.

In English class we were studying a book by Stephen Crane called *The Red Badge of Courage*. It was a great book all about a young soldier who fought for the Union Army during the Civil War. But when we got to a part in class when Mr. Burton explained about why he ran away, things got pretty bad.

"You see," Mr. Burton said, "the young soldier has never faced fire before, and he spends a lot of time wondering what he'll do when he's faced with battle. But when the test comes, it catches him off guard. The real thing isn't like thinking about the matter. I think we ought to learn something from this story, about how to expect difficult and dangerous times. I suppose we ought to learn there's no way to be sure what we'll do in a dangerous situation. Yes?"

Roy Prince was one of the guys in school who rodeoed. He'd been running with Jack Monroe ever since Jack had come. Roy was a short, husky guy, with pig eyes and a silly grin on his face most of the time. He glanced at me and said with a snicker, "I reckon we better ask ole Barney there about runnin' away. He took one look at a little old Brahman bull and run like a scared rabbit, didn't you now, Buck?"

The room got quiet. I guess they were waiting for me to blow up, or at least answer him, but what was there to say? Mr. Burton, wimp that he usually was, came to my rescue—in a way.

"Now, Roy, you mustn't deal in personalities. We've all heard about Barney's loss of face, but he has many good qualities. Not everyone is gifted with courage."

Wasn't *that* a nice way to put it!

After class, Debra tried to stop me in the hall, but I wouldn't listen. All I could think of was that she'd seen me run! I pulled away from her, ran out and got in the truck and went spinning out of the parking lot fast enough to merit a ticket.

I had just gotten to the Interstate when I saw the blue lights blinking in my rearview mirror. It was Chief Tanner. I pulled over and just sat there sulled up like a big Bullfrog. Chief came to my window and looked in at me, but I didn't say a word. Finally he sighed and said, "Barney, I know you're feeling like the President of the Poor Me Club, but you gotta pull out of it."

"What for?" I mumbled, not looking him in the eye. "Everybody knows I'm chicken!"

"No, they don't!" he snapped angrily. He took me by the shoulder and said, "There's only one guy in this town whose opinion you got to worry about."

"You, I guess?"

"No, *you*, Barney. You're gonna be the kind of guy you think you are. If you've decided to be a wimp and a quitter, why, I guess nobody can stop you. But it's your say."

"Easy for you to talk, Chief. You weren't the one who ran away with a million people watching you!"

"Son, everybody's got his own private bull. Yours is getting on the back of a bucking Brahman. For some it's high places. For others it's taking a final exam. And we all run away sometimes."

I knew he was trying to help, but I'd just built a wall about a hundred feet high around myself. I could hear what he was saying, but it didn't get *inside*. "You gonna give me a ticket for reckless driving?" I asked.

He sighed and said, "No. But you better snap out of this funk, son. You got a lot of responsibility with two younger brothers. You've done better than any boy I ever saw, but you're headed for real trouble acting like this."

He left and I went home. Everybody tried

to talk to me that week, including Coach Littlejohn. I guess it was the only time I wouldn't listen to him, but I shut him out, too. That was the worst week of my life. I got so mean I kicked Tim! I really loved that dog—he was like a human being, and he was the best dog in the world, but when a guy gets mean, he just *looks* for ways to act rotten!

The worst was what I did to Joe. If I made my list of the sweetest people in the world, my brother Joe would be right at the top. He always reminded me of Mom. She'd been gone for a couple of years, but I could never forget how she could take the hurt out of anything. It could be a cut or a bruise or something physical and when I'd gotten afraid or angry or whatever, I can remember how all she had to do was just hold me close and talk to me and it was all right!

Joe was like that. I liked to think about what a great man he was going to be when he grew up, because even though he couldn't read, he was the one everybody in his class came to when they were in a jam. He was the one of us Buck boys who never seemed to lose his cool, who was always ready to laugh with Jake and me when we had something good happen, or who could just sit down by us when we were low, and without a word make us know that he was hurting with us.

Would you believe I hit him? Well, I did! Oh,

not really a *hit*, but close enough.

I was sitting in a chair in the living room staring at the wallpaper, having a real pity party, and I guess Joe was trying to cheer me up. He'd made some sort of a puppet out of paper cups and tin cans and painted it to look like Slim Galliard, the skinny fellow who stuttered and helped us set up our garden. We all loved the guy, but he was so easy to make fun of!

Well, Joe made this puppet and then he sneaked up behind me and all of a sudden he dangled it in front of my face and yelled, "B–B–B–Barney, I–I–I g–g–g–got you!"

That nearly scared me to death because I was a million miles away. I jumped up and hollered and that tickled Joe, who thought he'd done a good job of cheering me up. Actually I was ashamed that I'd hollered like that. It reminded me too much of the last time I'd shown my yellow streak. That's when I reached out and gave Joe a shove. He fell over backward against the wall with a thud that must have hurt, and he stood there staring at me with his big blue eyes wide open and his mouth trembling.

It was the meanest thing I'd ever done, and I couldn't even say I was sorry! The tears gathered in Joe's eyes, and suddenly my own eyes were blinded. I whirled and ran out the door, down the steps, and out into the woods. I guess I was a little crazy. I could hear Joe calling out, "Barney, come back! Don't go, Barney!"

But I couldn't face him. I could see Joe's face even though my eyes were still blurred, but sometimes it didn't look like Joe's face at all.

It looked like Mom's face, and I could almost hear her saying something I'd heard her say ten thousand times, *You boys may do a lot of bad things, but if you love each other, that makes up for eveything!*

I ran as if a mad dog were after me, but finally I just ran out of air and had to stop. It was quiet, and all I could hear was the sound of my own hoarse breathing. Far off I heard a barn owl call, "Who!" and I almost answered, "It's me, Barney Buck, the one who runs away and who beats up on his little brother."

Well, what I did was just plain run away. It was about ten o'clock, one of those real warm summer nights when you can smell the fresh earth and hear a hundred sounds—skeeters humming, coyotes baying the moon, big bullfrogs like bass fiddles going *plunk* into the pond. The sky was lit up like a big pinball machine, sparkling and winking against the summer sky.

Every time I got down in the mouth, I made for the woods, and I hadn't gone over a mile before I heard Tim coming. He yelped a little, and then I knelt and caught him close as he jumped and bowled me over, trying to lick my face and nip at my feet at the same time.

I played with him, then stood up and said, "Let's go find us a real mean boar coon, boy!" We went quite a way, mostly over toward the river bottoms where I knew the coons were thick as warts on a toad. It was just for fun, even though we ran a bunch of them pretty hard.

I stayed out all night, then built a big fire. Tim and I just sat there and watched the fire and listened to the woods until nearly sunup. I was thinking about dragging myself back when I heard a voice calling me, "Boy! You there?"

I got up and saw Jim Bob walking into the light of my fire. "Jim Bob! How'd you ever find me?"

"Oh, you ain't as hard to track as some other varmints I've run to earth, boy!" He sat down slowly by the fire, groaned a little, then said, "My old bones is acting up a mite. You have some of this." He handed me a thermos that was full and heavy. "And I'll have some of *this!*"

"Cocoa!" I said when I pulled the cap off. It was always cold just before dawn, and I drank half of the jug not caring that it burned my throat. Then I took a breath and watched him sipping at a small jug. "That cocoa you got in your jug, Jim Bob?"

"What else?" he said, then grinned and took another sip. "I take a little wine for my stomach's sake, as the Good Book says."

We sat there and finally I asked, "Joe sent you to get me?"

"Said he'd feel better if I'd come find you."

"Guess he told you what I did!"

"Nope, but you been such a fool lately, whatever it was wouldn't surprise me a bit."

"You come out here to preach a sermon?"

"Naw, I ain't. Just to tell you what a jackass you're making out of yourself."

"Seems like everybody knows just how I ought to act," I said loudly.

He took another sip from his cup, then stared at me across the embers of the dying fire. Tim must have heard something stirring in the woods, because he lifted his head and said, "Wuff!" then slouched down again with his head on my knee.

I kept waiting for Jim Bob to talk, but he just sat there and stared at me. Finally, I couldn't stand it. "I know I'm acting dumb, Jim Bob, but I'm so–so *ashamed!* To run away like I did!"

Jim Bob kept staring at me, then gave me a real smile. I guess it was the first real one I'd ever seen on his face. It reminded me of the kind of smile Mom and Joe might've given me.

Then Jim Bob reached into his back pocket and took something out and handed it across the fire to me. "Wanted to show you this, boy."

It was something flat wrapped in a piece of

soft leather. I took it out and held it up to the firelight.

"Why, it's a prize buckle!" I held it closer and read the writing out loud, "All-around Cowboy."

"Why, I should have guessed you rodeoed, Jim Bob," I said. "Which rodeo was this for?"

"It's All-around Cowboy, Barney."

I stared at it, then looked across the fire at him. "You mean for the *national?*"

He nodded and said, "Yep. The whole shootin' match."

"Gosh!"

"I wanted you to see it, boy, because you're in a mess. And I wanted you to know just being afraid ain't the worst thing there is in this world."

I stared at him. "Were you afraid, Jim Bob?"

"Not of nothing in this world, except one thing. I could get on the meanest horse that ever upset me world, ride any, except one thing."

"What was it?"

He poked at the fire with a stick, and I thought for a long time he wasn't going to answer me. Then he looked up and said, "Bulldoggin' steers." He shook his head. "I dunno why it was, but I jest couldn't do it, boy! I was able to get out of it by bein' a top hand in every other event, but every night for years I woke up screamin' thinkin' I was falling right on top of a steer with horns sharp as razors and about ten feet long!"

"Did—did anybody find out? That you were *afraid, I mean?*"

"Thing is, boy, *that* didn't matter so much. I knew I was scared, and that was the worst of it!"

"But if no one knew. . . ."

"Well, *one* feller knew. Name was Casey Tibbs, an All-around Cowboy more than once. he k̶

"You told him, Jim Bob?"

"Didn't have to, boy. We was pretty close, and I reckon he liked me. So one day he just came up to me, this was at the Calgary Stampede, and I was doing pretty well, but ole Casey knew what was eatin' me. He came up ight after I won the bareback riding, and h̶ ̶sid, 'Puckett, you're gonna bulldog

"Oh, I cu̶s̶

own tater patch. Offered t̶ ̶pu̶

off." Jim Bob chuckled. "He jest stood there looking at me, and finally I just petered out. 'How'd you know I was skeered to bulldog, Casey?' I asked him.

" 'Cause you look at them steers just like I looked at bareback bucking horses when I first came up. I was scared green of them, and it takes one to know one! But you ain't gonna stay scared of them dumb cows. I'm gonna cure you just like I got cured,' he said."

"What did he do to get you cured, Jim Bob?"

He didn't answer, but took out his Skoal and filled his upper lip. Then he asked, "What you wanna know for, boy?"

"Why. . . ."

"You want somebody to wave a magic wand, give you a chest full of courage—like that silly lion in the pitcher show *The Wizard of Oz?*"

"Well, I gotta do *something!*"

He looked at me for a while, then said, "Barney, you remember the first week I come here, when we was walking behind the house out to the tater patch. Remember when that copperhead nearly got me in the calf?"

"Sure I do."

"What did you do to that snake?"

"Why, I just threw him out into the woods. That was all."

"Jest threw him out into the woods! What you done was reach out and pick that big snake up by the tail afore he could get me—and with your bare hands! Do you know, boy, that most everybody I know would nearly let theirselves be cut to pieces before they'd do a stunt like that?"

"Well, I just never have been afraid of snakes." I stretched the truth just a little.

"I know. But you are afraid of bulls. So that means you don't have to do nothing

about snakes, but you do about bulls. 'Cause
you got a lot of living to do, boy, and I don't
want you to wind up like me."

It sounded like a man who felt sorry for
himself, but Jim Bob wasn't a whiner. He was
just stating a fact, and it was the first and
last time I ever heard him say anything about
how hard his life had been.

"I–I don't know, Jim Bob. Looks like I'm
just a weakling when it comes to bulls. Not
much you can do about it."

"You're wrong, Barney," Jim Bob said. He
reached out and took the buckle, stared at it,
then said, "This is about all I got to show for
my whole life, boy. No family. No kids. No
wife. No home place or roots. Just this."

"Why, I was hoping you'd think of our
place as your home, Jim Bob."

He dropped his head and didn't say much.
Then he said, lifting his head, "That's real
handsome of you, boy. Real handsome. And I
maybe will do that, but you got to give me a
part in it."

I didn't really understand that. "What does
that mean?"

"Means I got to do more than set and
whittle, Barney. Man's got to have some
reason for being at a place. And the one thing
I can do is teach you to ride bareback, and
how not to be afraid of them bulls! If I can do
that and help that little Texas gal get her
horse, why, I reckon I'll feel a little bit better
about hanging it up."

I cleared my throat and asked, "You've never been—I mean you're not a. . . ."

He saw where I was headed. "You're maybe wonderin' about if I've ever trusted the Lord, ain't you, boy?"

"Well, yes, I am."

"No, I ain't never give God none of myself," he said in a quiet voice. "Maybe I'm sorry 'bout that now, but what sort of hairpin would live like the devil all his life and then when he's old and worn, go whining to God for mercy?"

"Well, there *was* one," I said.

"Yeah, that thief? I've thought about him a lot lately, boy. But it's too late for me. But if you'll let me help you right on this bull thing, why, it'll make me feel like I can shove my feet under your table and not be shamed."

I got up and walked over to him, and he got up, too. I stuck my hand out, and his bones felt small in my big palm. "I told someone once you might be an angel in disguise, Jim Bob. If you can get me over being a coward with those bulls, I'll have to say you fit the bill!"

He grinned, then scratched his head and spit into the fire. "Well, I been lots of things, boy, but this one may be the dad-gummest ripsnorter of the whole caboodle!" Then he took off his hat and threw it high into the air and cut loose with a screaming yell. I knew he'd done that many a time when he'd made a good ride in the arena!

"I takes off my hat," he said, "to the next champion bull rider of the universe! Or anywhere else for that matter!" He grinned, and then we started for home.

SIX

One Ton
of Trouble

"I'm not sure this is such a good idea, Jim
Bob." I felt a little shaky in the knees as I
stopped and went between the rails, then
stood up not twenty feet away from a herd
of Brahman bulls. They looked as big as
elephants, and every nerve in my body told
me to *run!*

Jim Bob was looking at me with a clinical
eye. "Boy, I want you to walk up to the
biggest, meanest critter you see in that bunch
and slap him on the rump."

"What!"

"Yep, that's what you want to do."

"But they'll stomp me!"

"Won't neither." He grinned. "Even if they
did, I don't expect it would plumb kill you.
Get on with it."

The sun was so hot that little flecks of
light reflected off the huge horns of the bulls.

Jim Bob had rousted me out of the hammock where I was taking a nap under the big catalpa tree in our front yard, saying, "Boy, it's time to educate you on them bulls!" Then he'd made me drive him in the pickup over to Wallace Steven's farm and led me to the pasture where the herd of registered Brahmans were kept.

I made myself put one foot in front of the other, but the closer I got, the more my heart beat like a big drum! I wiped the sweat out of my eyes and tried not to notice how badly my hands were trembling.

The biggest bull had a funny set of horns, one turned up and the other pointed down. He lifted his head as I got closer, then wheeled to face me, his head down and little grunts coming out of his chest.

"He don't weigh but a ton, boy, and you weigh maybe a hundred or so. Show him who's boss!"

The Brahman lowered his head, and I thought he was about to charge; so I just made my mind a blank and jumped at him. He threw his head up, and I hollered, "Get, you monster!" as loudly as I could. He tossed his head, then lumbered around. Right away I slapped his rump—which sent him galloping off at top speed.

As I watched the others trot off after him, I turned and said, "Gosh! He didn't even try to hurt me!"

"No, but then, he ain't no trained bucking

bull, neither," Jim Bob said. He squatted down on his heels. "What you got to do, boy, is get used to the animal. I want you to come out here every day and just get close to these bulls. It won't be the same as gettin' on a bucking bull, but pretty soon the *size* and the horns won't have no effect on you."

"Then what?"

"Then you try to get on one of the critters and ride him."

"Why is it I'm scared of a bull but not of a horse?"

"I dunno, boy. Jest happens that way. I reckon you've seen that a horse don't pay no never-mind to a man he bucks off, but a bull will go for him."

"Are they trained to do that—go for the rider, I mean?"

"No, they ain't. Just trained to buck." He leaned back on his heels and grinned at me, then spit out a wad of brown juice. "I don't think there's much to this here reincarnation business, but if there *was*, I'd want to come back as one of them bucking bulls."

I stared at him. "Why in the world would you want to do that?"

"Why, jest look at it, boy. A man who furnishes bucking stock to the rodeo has expensive animals. If he uses them too often, they get lazy and won't buck. That means he loses money. So the best bulls are only rode one time a week. You know how long a ride lasts at most?"

"Eight seconds?"

"Right! You know any job a man can get working eight seconds a week?"

We talked a long time, and before we got home, he said, "Boy, I'm gonna tell you something, although maybe I ought not to. I want to say you got what it takes to be a real rider."

"Oh, Jim Bob, you only saw me ride one time. I'm not big and strong like Jack Monroe!"

He snorted and said, "Strong? How many men you know are strong as a horse? Or as one of them bulls? Not any! Good ridin' is mostly balance, boy, and I saw you got that when you rode that Mankiller horse. You rode him like an old hand, and you ain't had no lessons at all. Now I'm not saying you're goin' to win the all-around award this year—or ever. But if you make up your mind, I can make a contender outta you."

I thought about that and said, "Gee, I'll try my best, Jim Bob. But I can't make any promises about–about, well. . . ."

" 'Bout bull ridin'? Well, don't fret. Jest let it come, boy. Do some of that prayin' if you got to, and listen to me. I reckon between me and the good Lord, we'll make a rider outta you right soon!"

That was just a small part of Jim Bob's plan for me! He got a list of every high school rodeo in our part of the world, and we just about ran the wheels off the pickup getting to them.

"You see how easy this is, boy?" he asked me when we were driving home after making three rodeos scattered all the way from Fort Smith, Arkansas, to New Boston, Texas.

"Easy! You call this *easy?*" I moaned. I had done pretty well, winning first place in Fort Smith and second in New Boston and Broken Bow. But I was tired, bruised, and about to fall over for lack of sleep.

"Why, boy, what if you was a roper? Or a bull dogger? You'd have to take your own horse. That'd mean a trailer and stopping every few hours to let the horse out of the box. No, this is the way! Jest have to get yourself to the arena."

I guess he was right, but my eyes were so gritty from lack of sleep that I went to sleep in class lots of times.

But things were better, you know? I made it up with Joe, who never was angry anyway. I got along with most people at school. Debra was a little cool, but she was busy with her horse and I just sort of thought after the rodeo season I'd make it up to her. Maybe I'd take her to Little Rock to see a movie or something big like that.

Well, maybe I ought to add that she was a little put out by the fact that Tater was going on most of the trips with Jim Bob and me. It was Jim Bob's idea. "Got to give that little

Texas gal something to hope for, boy!" he'd say.

"You still think we can let her ride that horse?" I asked.

"Got to do it, boy! Got to do it!"

Tater was doing pretty well, but she still looked sort of *lost*. She talked about Don Pedro all the time, and she had absolute faith that she'd get him.

"If I just had Don Pedro, Barney, why, it wouldn't be so bad—about my mom and all," she'd say.

One time we were sitting in the truck waiting for Jim Bob to pay my entrance fees for a rodeo in Malvern. I'd bought her a Coke and a burger from the concession stand, and she was nibbling at them and telling me about the horse. "Jim Bob says Don Pedro will be a champion, and he says he can show me how to cut two or three seconds off my time. Barney, it's cool tonight, isn't it?"

"Cool? Well, to tell the truth, I thought it was a little muggy, but I can get you an extra shirt. . . ."

"Oh, no, just sit close to me."

We went on talking, and I couldn't figure out how she was cold! *I* sure wasn't. I guess maybe girls feel things like that more than guys. She leaned against me and said, "Barney, I just don't know what I would have done if you hadn't come along. I mean, life was over!"

"Well, Tater, Jim Bob is really the one who's done his best for you."

"Sure, I know, but he's older, you know. A girl needs someone her own age to talk to. I feel closer to you than anybody I've ever known!" She leaned against me and suddenly reached up and kissed me.

I wasn't much for *kissing;* so I sort of pulled away and said, "Well, that's real nice, Tater. I guess you know how much all of us think of you."

"Do you *really?* Really and truly, Barney?"

"Well, sure, Tater."

"You mean you really think we have a *special* relationship?"

"Sure I do. . . ." I started to tell her how much Jake and Joe, and really all of us thought of her, but just then Jim Bob came back and said, "C'mon boy, I wanna tell you a few things about this horse. Been doin' a little askin' around."

I got out of the truck, and Tater said, "I feel a lot better now, Barney. I–I've wanted to hear you say it for a long time. See you after your ride."

"Sure," I said. I really didn't understand her, but Jim Bob was rattling along on how a horse named Blockbuster created a fuss in the chute. That made me forget all about Tater.

When I slid onto Blockbuster, I suddenly realized how caught up I'd gotten with bareback riding in a short time. As I slid my hand into the glove, then gripped the rigging, I suddenly realized that I wasn't even thinking about the crowd. I would have ridden the horse if there hadn't been a single person watching. I guess I was *hooked*, at least Jim Bob had said so.

There was that one second when I was gripping Blockbuster with my legs, and he was quivering all over, all muscle and nerves and out to get rid of me if he could. Then the gate swung open, and he went out like a cannonball!

One thing I'd learned, and that was if you don't *start* right, it's all over! I caught his rhythm, throwing my spurs up to his shoulder, and he just went straight up into the air. Then he did something no other horse I'd been on had ever done. He went high into the air and came down, but on *one foot!* The jolt ran all the way from my toes to the back of my neck! My head popped backward, then snapped forward, and the blood filled my head so that I had hardly any feeling at all. Somehow—and I don't know how I did it—I let my body fall forward with my arm out stiff to keep from touching the horse. I was headed off and got braced for the blow as the ground rose up to hit me.

Then Blockbuster outsmarted himself. He should have let well enough alone, but just as I was falling forward, he made another move that threw his front quarters up, and that broke my forward motion. Jim Bob said later that it looked like one of the slickest bits of riding anyone had ever seen. When I tried to tell him how it *really* was, he grinned and said, "Yeah? Well, that's the way it goes sometimes. But you made a great ride, boy."

I won first place, but to tell the truth, there wasn't much competition that night.

I nodded to the crowd when they applauded, then went back to the chutes where Jim Bob was taking the rigging off Blockbuster. He was looking pretty tired, and I said, "I think we ought to take a break, Jim Bob. I'm pretty tired."

He glanced at me, and I knew he saw through that. "You mean, you think I'm pretty tired, ain't that the way of it, boy?" He got the rigging free, and we went over to where the bulls were being loaded into the chutes for the bull riding. "You about ready to crawl on one of them?" he asked suddenly.

I stared at him, then at one of the bulls that had just slammed his horns against the sides of the chute. My stomach did a roll, but I didn't answer right off. Instead, I walked over and stared at the Brahman. He was a fierce-looking bull, with the whites of his eyes showing. When he rattled the rails with a volley of tremendous kicks, I thought, *What if one of those kicks caught a fellow right in the face?* But even though my stomach wasn't too settled and my hands were sweaty, I found myself actually *considering* the idea!

"Don't look impossible, does it?" Jim Bob said quietly.

"I guess it doesn't."

"I entered you in the bull riding, boy." He saw my head snap around to stare at the bull, then said, "Don't do it if you don't want to."

I felt as if I were in a hollow jar somewhere with all the noise filtered out. I was dry-mouthed and my voice was a little thin. "Why'd you do that?"

"I think you're ready, boy."

We stood there, and I suddenly knew I was going to do it. I sort of *had* to do it, somehow! "All right, I'll do it."

Jim Bob suddenly gazed at me, and the biggest grin I'd even seen lit up his face. He smacked me on the shoulder with his gnarled hand and said, "Son of a gun! I *knowed* you was a rider!"

Things went fast after that and all too soon I found myself easing down on one ton of meanness. His name was Trouble, and he was fairly quiet in the chute. But when the gate opened, he leaped into the arena like a big cat and made one wild circle. Then off I went. It was probably the quickest ride in the history of rodeo!

I hit the ground, rolled over, and was on my feet in about three seconds, but Trouble had already wheeled, found me, and lunged right at me with needle-sharp horns!

I could see he had me, but there was a

flash of movement over to my right, and suddenly, Trouble wheeled and made for whatever it was. I scrambled out of the arena, falling on my head with no shame whatsoever. When I got up, I saw a clown drawing that bull off by waving a red bandana in his face.

"Well, you done rode a bull, ain't you, boy!" Jim Bob had come up to stand by me, and I said, "Not very long, Jim Bob."

"Ain't no matter, boy! You rode him! And that's what. . . ." He broke off suddenly and turned pale as a piece of paper. His eyes rolled up showing the whites, and he began falling over backward!

"Jim Bob!" I said. "What's wrong?" I dragged him over to some Coke boxes and sat him down on one, but he felt boneless as a piece of liver. I held him up, and several of the cowboys came running. "Get a doctor!" I said. Right then he moved his head, and his eyes flew open. He seemed to come to himself all at once, and he pulled away from me.

"Don't need no doctor, boy!" he said sharply. "Jest get me outta this place."

"But. . . ."

"Don't argue with me!"

Well, I got him out and we got to the truck. He let me hold onto him, but as soon as he sat down, he seemed to be all right. "Just a bad case of indigestion. Had it lots of times. Now you go pick up that prize money, and we'll go on to the house."

I did as he said, but I made up my mind we'd have to cut down on some of the hard runs we were making. We got home and when I let Tater out, she hugged me and said, "I'm so *glad* you told me how you feel, Barney! It's good to have somebody who cares. And Debra will understand."

"Understand *what?*" I mumbled. I was played out and worried about Jim Bob; so when she gave me a big smile, I was just glad to be able to cheer the poor girl up.

The next day there was bad news.

Debra met me as I got out of the pickup, and I thought she looked a little odd. Her eyes were sort of squinty and her lips were thin. There was a little wrinkle between her eyes, and she talked in a sort of tense voice. "I got the word on your new *relationship* from Tater," she said.

"What?"

Then tears rose up in her eyes, and she said, "I do think you might have told me yourself."

"Told you *what,* Debra?"

"Oh, you don't have to act dumb! Tater *explained* it all to me very carefully! Well, I guess I am a little thick-headed. But even *I* know what you've been trying to tell me lately."

"Debra, what are you . . . ?"

"Oh, well, if you want me to say it—Tater told me how you feel like that you and I have been too close lately. But you and she are just *right* for each other. In her own words."

I tried to recall what Tater had said, but I'd been too tired to listen. Now I was trying to say something, but Debra just said, "You can go ahead and say something like, 'But we'll always be good friends, Debra!' " Then she just ran away and left me standing there.

Wasn't that just peachy!

I either had to hurt a poor girl who was an orphan and needed friends as bad as anybody I ever saw, or else lose Debra!

Well, that was bad news numero uno.

The second tidbit was when Jake came up to me as soon as I got home. He had that look on his face that always meant that he had an "operation" of some kind going. "Barney, our troubles are over! I have a plan!"

I sat down slowly and listened to his plan about winning the Great Race.

The fact that I sat there and listened to him shows you what a terrible mental condition I had developed! You'd think I would've learned by then!

SEVEN
The Great Race

Every summer in Cedarville we have the
Festival of the Three Rivers. The name comes
from the three small streams that all gather
in or near our town, and the festival is about
like a hundred others around the state. It has
cooking contests, craft booths, a few carnival
rides, competitions for horseshoe pitching,
egg-throwing, tobacco-juice spitting, but most
of the attention is focused on the Great Race.

Actually, the Great Race is in three stages:
boating, running, and bicycling. The
contestants have to ride in boats down a
stretch of the Caddo River in the first part.
The thing is, since it's the Festival of the
Three Rivers, the boats have to have three-
man teams. No motors are allowed, according
to the rules. The boats must be "manually"
powered. Then the three men have to run

from the landing side on the river to the top of Brown's Bluff, which is the highest spot in the county. That's a three-man event, too, and the three have to maintain contact—hold hands—to the top of the bluff.

Brown's Bluff overlooking the town has a winding hairpin road that goes up the sheer sides of it on the west face. The teams have a bicycle made for three at the top of the bluff where they begin the race, and they finish up on Main Street.

All the teams are sponsored by local businessmen who also put up the prize money. It's a pretty big amount—$1,000 for first place, $500 for second, and $250 for third.

Joe was all excited as they started explaining to me how we were going to win first prize and get Tater's horse.

"Wait a minute, you guys," I said. "Don't you know that a lot of guys have had a team for *years* doing nothing but training for the Great Race?"

"Sure, we know that," Joe said, "but they don't have what we have!"

"Which is what?"

"Which is two *great* inventions," Jake said waving his hands around wildly. "Joe has come up with two really amazing things!"

"Inventions? What kind of inventions? You have to use a boat, and you have to have a three-man bicycle. That's all there is to it."

"Ah!" Jake grinned and tapped his head

with a stubby forefinger. "That's why we'll win, Barney! Nobody ever *thought* about a different kind of boat or a different kind of bicycle!"

I stared at them, then said, "Well, let's have it. What have you got?"

"Come on, Joe, let's show him."

Jake led the way to Joe's workshop, which was just an old chicken house which we'd made weather tight and got electricity to. I usually kept up with Joe's activities, but going to so many rodeos had kept me too busy.

"There she is—Swiftwater!" Joe said proudly. "How do you like her, Barney?"

What I saw was a twelve-foot johnboat with three bicycles fastened together in the middle of it. "What in the world . . . !" I started to ask, but Joe ran around, pointing out how it worked.

"See, Barney, all the sprockets drive this chain, and the chain's just fixed her into this gear. See?"

"And what does that do?" I asked, a bit skeptically.

"It turns the propeller, see here?" He showed me a single propeller that exited from the back of the boat and was sealed in with a bushing and gasket.

"Look, Barney!" Jake shouted. "See how she works!" He got into the boat, which was resting on two sawhorses, and began peddling wildly. The little propeller spun along, and

Jake said, "Boy! When all three of us get to peddling, this baby will fly!"

"But—they won't ever allow this thing!" I said.

"They'll *have* to, Barney." Jake grinned and whipped out a paper from his hip pocket and read aloud: "No motors will be allowed. All boats will be manually powered." Then he shoved it under my nose and asked with a shrill voice, "Well, this is manually powered, ain't it? There ain't no motor, is there?"

"Well, no, I guess not," I said. "How fast will this thing go?"

"Well, we haven't actually tested her yet," Joe said hurriedly, "but the thing is, Barney, your legs are lots stronger than your arms, you see? So if the other teams are using their arms and we're using our legs, why, we'll have to win!"

I stared at the boat and it made sense. "I think you may be right. We can give it a trial this afternoon. Ought to be able to find out something."

"It'll work, Barney, I know it will!" Joe beamed. "Now, look at this!" He pulled an old tarp off of something over against the wall, and I blinked my eyes at the sight of it.

"What is *that?*" I gasped.

"Why, it's our Rough Rider Special!" Jake said proudly. "Ain't it a doozie!"

I'd never seen anything like it! It was a bicycle—of a sort. Anyway it had two wheels and handlebars. But that's when it stopped

looking like any bicycle I ever saw! In the
first place it must have weighed at least two
hundred pounds. It was made of a heavy
steel frame that stretched out nearly eight
feet. The wheels were heavy-duty truck
wheels with massive tires and large shocks.
On top of the thing were three seats made
out of heavy plate, not bicycle seats but wide
affairs with cushions.

"It's–it's–I don't know what to say," I said
lamely. "There aren't any pedals! How does
this thing *go*? And who in the world could
even pick it up?" I asked tugging at it.

"Oh, we won't have to *pedal*, Barney," Joe
said.

"Not pedal? What do we do then? We do
have to finish the race, you know."

Then they told me the Master Plan.

"That is *insane!*" I said when they'd laid it
all out. "In the first place, they probably
won't let us use this thing. In the second
place, the thing is too heavy to handle. In the
third place, everybody in town thinks we're a
little strange *now.* Imagine what they'll think
if we show up with this thing!"

"We can worry about that on the way to
buy Don Pedro for Tater," Joe said with a
smile.

That caught me up short. Actually the idea
wasn't too bad. I walked around the two
vehicles trying to find something to say.
Finally, I shook my head. "I guess we can give

it a try. What have we got to lose?"

I think General Custer said that just before he led his troops into the battle at Little Big Horn.

On the first day of June, the Great Race began with a great uproar—from the other teams.

I'd expected a challenge on the boat and the Rough Rider Special, but things got downright mean!

Tad Dooley and his brother, Tim, were the loudest. Their trio had won the Great Race two years running and were all set for an easy win. They were all ex-football players and kept in shape all the time. Tad, the oldest, was red in the face as he told Chief Tanner, who happened to be chief judge, "Why, you don't have the face to tell me you're going to let them crazy Bucks use them things!"

Chief just handed him a copy of the rules and said, "Show me where they're against the rules, Tad."

"I don't care about your rules, Chief! They're making a show out of a great tradition!"

"Yeah, and we ain't gonna stand for it!" Tim snarled. He didn't have any neck, and he looked a lot like the Brahman I'd ridden the past week, except he wasn't as good-looking.

Well, they argued and got even redder in

the face and cussed, but at the end we were allowed to register the boat and the Rough Rider Special. It took all of us with some help from our friends to get the monstrous Rider onto the bed of the pickup, and Coach Littlejohn agreed to take a crew and get it to the top of the bluff.

"Don't know why you bother, though," he said thoughtfully. "Those Dooley boys are great runners. You can't run against them and win."

"We can make up for that with Swiftwater and Rough Rider," I said, without really believing it.

"How in the world are you going to make those hairpin turns on this thing?" Coach asked. "If it falls on you, it'll break every bone in all your bodies."

"We have a plan," I said, trying to look mysterious. I didn't succeed, though. I just came across looking silly.

It was a perfect day for the race, and I guess everybody in the whole county was there. We got in the pickup and rode out to the river where all the boats were lined up. Swiftwater stuck out like a sore thumb. There were seven small light johnboats and twelve canoes and two rafts that some guys had entered as a joke.

Everyone got into his boat and waited for the mayor to give the signal. He pulled a pistol out of his coat pocket and pointed it in the air. Then he let it fly. When we heard the loud *bang*, all of us started paddling like crazy!

The banks were lined with people for the first five hundred yards. As the banks got rough with timber, only a few people could be spotted along the way. The Caddo was a pretty stream, free flowing and full of fish, but we didn't have time to look at it.

Every day for a week we'd gone out at dusk to a secluded section of the Ouachita River and practiced, and I was convinced we'd win the boat race. Actually it was no contest!

We went sailing along, and within a hundred yards we were five boat lengths in front. After half a mile we were out of sight of the other crafts.

"Don't slow down," I said. "We'll have some of them breathing down our necks before the run is over!"

We made the race quicker than anyone ever had. Archie Caples, the county sheriff, was waiting at the landing. He stared at us with unbelieving eyes when we rounded the bend and pulled into the bank. He called out our time, but we had already grabbed hands and were making for the top of the bluff.

"Let's take it easy," I said. "It's a long uphill run. We'll have to pace ourselves."

Actually I wasn't worried about myself. I'd spent so many hours running dogs in the woods I thought I could keep ahead of the Dooleys and all the rest. Jake wasn't in bad shape, either, but Joe was just too young. He wasn't athletic; so I knew he was the weak link in our plan.

We'd gotten about halfway to the bluff when I heard a shout. "There they are," I said. "We'll have to step it up."

Joe did pretty well until we got about a quarter up the slope; then he started gasping for breath.

"We'll have to slow down," I said, gritting my teeth. I guess we'd all known this would happen, but there was no way to help it.

It wasn't long before we had somebody coming up behind us. "We got 'em now, Tim," I heard Tad holler, and they caught up with us within a hundred yards. "You wasn't so smart after all, you Bucks!" Then they pulled on by and went out of sight in a bend in the trail.

"I–I can't go any faster, Barney!" Joe gasped.

The top was only about a hundred yards, but five other teams passed us before we pulled ourselves up the last stretch and staggered to the Rough Rider.

"We can still do it!" I gasped. "Get this thing going!" We all three pushed and tugged until the Rough Rider started rolling down the hill. It moved very slowly, but finally it picked up speed and Joe managed to crawl up into his seat with some help by Jake. Then Jake hopped on and said, "Get on quick, Barney!"

I managed to hop astride the machine just as the thing *really* took off, and we were on our way!

"There's the Dooleys—down there!" Jake hollered, and sure enough I glanced down in time to see them go sailing toward one of the hairpin turns. Several other teams were between us and them, but we were approaching the first turn and it was a critical moment—all our hope lay in what happened next!

When Jake and Joe had first explained how the Rough Rider could win, it sounded fairly possible. The plan was that instead of following the road, we would simply turn off and go straight down the side of the mountain.

"But we can't do that!" I had said. "That mountain is filled up with briars and scrub brush. Why, it would claw us to pieces!"

"No, because we'll mount a brush cutter on the Rough Rider," Joe had said.

The brush cutter was a massive fixed blade mounted on the front of the Rough Rider. It had been honed razor sharp by Joe with a grinder. With the tremendous weight of the Rough Rider, the blade would cut a path through the brush as we sailed right down the slope.

Well, that was a great *theory*, but now it was time to test it! We were going so fast the road under our heavy tires was blurred, and the small trees and bushes beside the road were a green blur. The Rough Rider was actually out of control, but there was no way to do anything else but carry out our plan.

"Hang on, you guys!" I shouted. "We're going down the slope!"

As we hit the first turn, we all leaned to our left as we had planned. We were going far too fast to make that hairpin turn; so what we did was go crashing through the underbrush at the turn. We hit with such a crash that I bit my lip and tasted blood, but there was no time to think about that. "Hang on! Hang on!" I screamed.

If there had been any big trees we'd have been killed, I guess. There was no time to steer. All we could do was just hope we could keep the Rough Rider from going into a ravine, and we'd been out to the bluff several times checking for that.

The blade seemed to be working, because none of the heavy bushes we sailed through did more than slap at us. All of us were wearing crash helmets and goggles, of course.

Just then we ran into the first leg of the road that had turned back on the slope. We nearly went down when the front tire hit the solid slab, but the heavy shocks took most of the bump.

What it did do was scare the sap out of a team of riders who were almost run down by the Rough Rider! I heard a scream and caught just a glimpse of a waving bunch of arms and legs as a cycle went down and over the side

in a mad effort to steer clear of the Rough
Rider. I guess it must have been pretty grim
to look up and see a thing like us—with a
blade five feet long mounted on the front of a
monstrous machine gleaming in the sun!

But we were off the road with a crash into
the brush and hurtling toward the next open
space. As we sailed through a clear spot, I
saw the Dooleys. Tad glanced up toward us. I
guess he must have heard us crashing
through the brush, unless he were deaf!

"Look out!" I screamed at them. "Get out of
the way!" We hit the road about fifty yards
in front of them, and they weren't in any
danger, but I guess Tad got spooked. He tried
to weave to one side, and when he went too
far, they went into a spin. I caught a glimpse
of another mess of arms and legs flailing like
a mad octopus!

"We got 'em!" Jake shouted. "We can't lose!
We're in front!"

I thought so, too. But right then we hit a
ditch we'd missed finding on our survey. It
wasn't too deep, maybe about a foot, but it
almost wrenched the handles out of my
hands. I felt something go loose in the
steering, and all of a sudden I realized that a
pin had sheared! We were flying down the
side of a mountain on a machine that we had
no control over!

"Get ready to jump!" I screamed. "The
steering is out!"

But I knew that to leave the Rough Rider

would be like jumping off a train into a pile of cactus! We'd just have to pray and hope that nothing got in our way!

"Joe!" I screamed. "Are there any brakes on this thing?"

"Sorry, Barney!" Joe said. "I didn't think we'd need any."

Well, we made it down the slope without getting killed—which was a pretty good trick! As soon as we hit the flats, trouble really started!

"Look out, Barney!" Jake screamed. He was peering around me, and he saw the same thing I did—a fence and an orchard of young apple trees!

"Hang on! We're going through the fence!" I hollered. It was just a picket fence, but it splintered into toothpicks when we sailed through it.

I'll tell you about that orchard. It belonged to Mr. Robert Harrington. He didn't have any kids; so he spent all his time and money on that orchard. He'd had the trees sent from somewhere in Europe and had planted them when they were just switches, watering them individually. If any boy ever got *near* one of those trees, he got a load of birdshot!

"Maybe we'll go *between* 'em, Barney!" Joe shouted.

I thought for a minute he was right. After all they were planted about twenty-five feet apart to give them room to grow, and with all that space, it'd be more likely to miss them, right?

We didn't miss the trees.

No, we swerved, and that Rough Rider acted as if it were hungry for apple trees! We hit the first one, then went right on down the row—clip—clip—clip. Like a big scythe we wiped out a whole row of those trees.

Just as we were approaching the fence on the far side, I caught a glimpse of Mr. Harrington leaning over to put some fertilizer on one of the young trees. He was pretty deaf; so he didn't hear us coming until we were right on top of him.

When he looked up, his eyes got big and he made a big *O* with his mouth. Then he did a back flip and got up running.

I guess the Rough Rider was too much for him.

We went crashing through the fence and ran right through Widow Pennington's yard. She'd probably just hung all her washing out, and the blade of the Rough Rider clipped off all five wires. Most of them got caught in the blade so we were trailing a long flag of underwear that fluttered and flapped in the breeze as we went rushing through Silas Heaton's chicken farm.

Mr. Heaton thought about as much of his prize white Dominickers as Mr. Harrington thought of his apple trees. He was out scattering feed as we rambled right through the middle of his best layers. The little chicken wire didn't even make the Rough Rider hesitate; we just went through like a huge bowling ball scattering chickens so far and wide it looked like a snowfall!

I don't think we killed many, but Mr. Heaton said most of them didn't lay an egg for a month!

"Hey! I think we're OK, you guys!" I shouted. "There's the finish line!"

Sure enough we hit the last slope and were on our way down Main Street! There was the finish line! We'd done it!

Unfortunately, the County Clerk, Berry White, was out riding his little purple moped. He had just turned off Sixth Street onto Main—right in front of us. He looked up and turned pale, then whipped the little moped to his right and started chugging madly toward the finish line!

He looked over his shoulder, and screamed, but there was no way he could get out of the way of the Rough Rider. Crowds lined both sides of the street, and he had to keep going. Finally, he found an opening and ran his moped right into Mrs. Maples's Beauty Shop where he usually got his hair done. She never would let him come back after that, though.

Well, we sailed right through the tape, and a cheer went up!

We had won! But we hadn't *stopped!*

No, we plowed right on, and finally hit a bump, which turned the Rough Rider into a place that Mr. Charles Taylor, the high school biology teacher, had rented to use for his part-time business—which was collecting specimens for the government.

We crashed through the front door and wiped out just about every cage and case he had.

Well, a lot of people came rushing in to see what had happened to us, but they went rushing out even faster.

The thing is, most of Mr. Taylor's specimens got loose. His specimens included about a hundred mice, quite a few snakes—most of them harmless, but a few pit vipers—and one timber wolf.

You might say there were mixed emotions as the specimens going out met the people going in.

Well, by the time the people whose trees we'd ruined, whose washings we'd run off with, whose chickens we'd scared out of laying had got to town to file complaints, and Mr. Taylor had made his speech, and about five hundred people who'd been scared out of their wits by the specimens, and most of the teams we'd left up on the bluff had arrived all scratched up—well, I guess Chief Tanner was putting it pretty mildly when he said, "I don't know what this town did for excitement until you Bucks came to town!"

EIGHT
The Bet

"Well, Barney," Chief Tanner sighed, "I'm afraid that by the time you get through paying for the apple trees you smashed, the washing you scattered all over Clark County, the bill for eggs that chickens didn't lay, and add to that all the snakes, wolves, and assorted varmints you let loose on an innocent town. . . ."

"I guess you're trying to tell me not to expect to keep any of the prize money, right, Chief?"

"Well, that's about it, I reckon, but the way you ought to look at it is you could of got sued for every dime you got!"

"Which would be about nine dollars at most," I said.

Tater and I had been sitting out on the front porch when the Chief had driven up.

She had been spending most of her spare time with us, sticking close to Jim Bob and rattling on about that horse of hers. She stayed so close to me that I was afraid to step without stepping on her. I knew she'd been counting on enough money from the festival prize to at least make a down payment, but Chief gave us the bad news.

"But—you mean there won't be *any* prize money?" she asked, turning to look at Chief with a tragic expression.

"Well, I'm afraid not enough to do any good," he said. He'd been keeping up with Tater's problems, just as he seemed to keep up with everyone else's. I don't think a cat had a litter that Chief didn't know about!

Tater's lip trembled, and she bit it quickly. Shaking her head, she turned to leave. "I'm never going to have a horse!"

"Don't give up, Missy," Chief Tanner said as she went slowly across the yard and started into the woods. "I seen this here Barney Buck pull some hot potatoes outta the fire!" He raised his voice and added, "Just trust in the Lord and Barney Buck, Missy!"

"I wish you wouldn't say things like that, Chief. She's had enough disappointments. No sense giving her another," I said.

"Barney, I meant it. You done some things I swore couldn't be done more than once! Don't give up on this one." He stared at the opening in the trees where she had disappeared. "Where's she headed?"

"Jim Bob spends lots of time fishing in the pond. She goes out and tells him she's going to get Don Pedro."

"Ain't said nothin' about moving on, has he?"

"Nope."

"Well, if you want me to move him off. . . ."

"No, don't do that. He doesn't eat as much as a bird and we got the room. Besides, where would he go?"

Chief Tanner stared at me with a funny expression on his face. "For a Yankee boy, you sure got a lot of southern hospitality." He grinned, then said, "Well, I got to get back to town. Sorry about all the prize money, Barney. Don't let it throw you."

He drove off, and I ambled down the path to talk to Jim Bob. It was pretty hot, but not too hot to go on a little coon hunting trip. I knew Jim Bob would say I needed to go to a rodeo somewhere or other, but I was pretty worn down. We'd gone to four already that week, and I'd done OK, but not as good as Jim Bob said I should have done.

Just as I expected, Jim Bob was telling Tater about show horses. He had a long cane pole baited up with catalpa worms, and he jerked a big pumpkin seed perch that glistened blue, red, and gold with lots of orange in the sun. He slipped it off the hook, then looked up and saw me.

"Boy, you got us another rodeo?"

I sat down beside him and asked, "You

trying to wear me out, Jim Bob? I'm tired!"

He slipped a worm on his hook, spit some amber tobacco juice on it, and snorted, "Tired! What in the blue nanny you got to be *tired* about?"

"Why'd you spit on that worm?" I asked, trying to change the subject.

" 'Cause it makes the fish bite better! Now, when we goin' out again?"

"Oh, that's just a superstition," I said.

"You young whippersnapper! Now, you got to ride every time you can, boy. Ain't gonna learn to ride a horse out of no book!"

Tater had been standing up, tossing stones into the pond, but she came over and sat down close beside me. She took my arm and looked up at me. "Barney," she said, "Jim Bob says if you'll listen to him, you can make lots of prize money—enough to buy Don Pedro."

I made a mistake then, a pretty bad one.

The way Tater was hanging on to me all the time and sort of acting as if she *owned* me—well, it was getting on my nerves! So I just pulled away from her, stood up, and said a little bit harder than I meant to, "Tater, you got to quit that!"

"Quit what?" she asked. She had the hurt look on her face she sometimes had. "What'd I do, Barney?"

"You got to quit that hanging onto me all the time. And you got to stop depending on me to get that horse!"

She looked up at me, then turned and

stared out at the pond. It was real quiet, and I wished I'd kept my mouth shut. Finally, she said so softly I almost missed it, "I'm sorry, Barney. I won't do it again."

She turned and went down the path to the house, and I almost called out to her, but I couldn't think of anything to say.

"Fine work, boy!" Jim Bob said. He spat into the water and added, "You like to hurt little gals that don't have no folks?"

"Don't you start on me, Jim Bob! I'm up to here in advice about how to treat that kid!"

The cork Jim Bob had on his line disappeared with a solid *thunk*. Maybe he'd snagged a big bass. Anyway, he didn't even move, except to turn his grizzled old head up to stare at me. For a long time the only noise was a blue jay scolding over in the pear orchard. The longer that silence went on, the more my conscience cut me up like a bunch of sharp knives. Finally, I couldn't stand it any longer.

"All *right*. So I'm a monster!" I kicked a chunk of dead wood and nearly hurt my toe, and for some reason I blamed Jim Bob for that. "Now, that ought to make you happy! Now will you pull that stupid fish in!"

Jim Bob glanced at the cork, which was zinging around like mad. Then he said, "Why, boy, it don't eternally matter if I get that fish out or not. If I do, that's fine. If I don't, why, I guess we got a freezer full. So it jest don't matter much." With that, he lifted the fish out—a huge, slab-sided goggle-eye. He took it off the hook, stared at it, then suddenly tossed it back into the pond and watched it go scooting under a big log.

"Why'd you do that?" I asked.

"Like I said, boy, it don't matter about that fish." He stood up, and I was surprised again as I always was about how small he was. Of course I was so tall I made most folks look short, but he was thin, too. When you saw him from the rear, he looked so thin and short, you'd mistake him for a young boy.

But his face was old with lines around the eyes, and his neck was crinkled and you could see his stringy neck muscles. He wasn't as tanned as he'd been when he first came. He was still a little dark, but underneath that, he was sort of pale. I'd noticed, too, that he held his mouth sort of funny, as if he had a toothache and didn't want to let on.

Now he let out a huge sigh and said, "Boy, I told you, it don't matter about that fish. But it does matter about that gal."

"Sure, I know, Jim Bob. But I just can't. . . ."

"Now, that little gal," he said softly as the breeze that was blowing the cattails in the pond, "why, she's jest 'zactly in the shape I was in when I was her age. Been beat around and shoved from pillar to post. Nobody to call my own, not a soul. Tired of trying to smile. And I tell you true, boy, I got to the point, if one more thing—jest *one!*—had come on me, why I would have plain given up." He turned and started down the path, picking up a string of panfish as he went. He moved slowly and I slowed down to walk with him.

"But I can't get the money for that horse!" I said.

"Maybe you can't, but you didn't have to pull away from that gal. And you didn't have to sound like a bill collector tellin' her to keep her hands off you."

I turned red and short of breath the way I do when I feel guilty. I followed him toward the house and finally said, "I–I guess you're right about that, Jim Bob, but you got to understand. Look, Tater—well, she *likes* me—I mean, she wants a boyfriend."

"Well, whut's wrong with that?"

"Nothing, only, well, it's just not gonna be *me*. And I can't let her think it will be."

He didn't say a word, and when we got to the table out behind the house where we clean fish, I got the knife out of the drawer and gave it to Jim Bob. I tried to tell him how bad it would be if she thought I was *serious* about her, but then found out I wasn't.

Jim Bob did all the cleaning. He took a fish out of the basket with his left hand, cut down with one motion, then put the knife down and pulled the head and the entrails out with one jerk and tossed the fish to me. I took a spoon in my right hand, held the fish flat on the left, and with about four passes, I had the bream free of scales. It took us about forty-five seconds, and if there's a better fish on this earth to eat than perch, I'd like to find out about it.

He listened while I talked. After we were through, he put the fish into a bucket of water and said, "I ain't got no answers, boy. If I did, I wouldn't be a broken-down old rodeo bum. Which is what I am. But I gotta say one thing to you." He pulled at my arm with his gnarled hand and looked me right in the eyes. "I done lots of pretty bad stuff in my time, boy, but the part that bothers me the most, you know what it is?"

"No, Jim Bob."

"It's them times I could've helped somebody, maybe kept him from goin' over the edge. And I jest plain didn't do it!"

He looked real bad. I figured he never had gotten over that virus. I stared at him, and it really got to me. He hadn't given me any *reasons* why I ought to be different with Tater, but those little knives that cut me up inside from time to time were pretty busy.

"Well, Jim Bob," I finally said, "I guess there's something to that. And I'll try. I really will. You see if I don't!"

He suddenly smiled, and it was good to see the lines on his face break up a little.

"I betcha you will, too, you son-of-a-gun!"

Well, I went right at it. We took the fish to the kitchen, and I found Joe and Jake playing Monopoly in the living room with Tater. Joe was winning as usual. I could tell that Tater was ignoring me on purpose, and that got the little knives busy.

I went over to where they were sitting on the floor and plopped down between Joe and Tater. Tater didn't have but two or three pieces of property; so I gave her a hug and smiled at her. "You need me, Tater. That little thug will cut your throat at this game. But I can get him into line for you."

Joe looked up and said in surprise, "But, Barney, you never beat me at this game."

"Course not! I've been *letting* you win, punk! Now I'm about to let you have it with both barrels!"

"Is that right, Barney?" Joe said all wide-eyed. "I never knew that!"

He'd have believed me if I'd said the sun was made of Jell-O, but I didn't let up. "I'm going in partners with Tater, and you're a dead duck. You, too, Jake!"

"Better join up with me!" Jake grinned. "I got a pretty good chance. Tater ain't got a prayer!"

"Oh, yeah? You just watch yourself, brother!" I said.

Well, it was strange! I was no good at all at the silly game. Jake and Joe both cleaned my plow easy. But that night I went at it like I was fighting fire. I rolled and roared and didn't give Jake or Joe one minute's peace. I took turns with Tater moving the little piece around the board, and you know what? I got those two so rattled that they made a lot of dumb moves and we *won!*

I grabbed Tater and picked her up like a doll, spinning her around the room in a crazy dance. "See there, Tater, what we can do when we set our minds at it. Ain't *nothing* we can't do! That right, partner?"

I set her down and smiled at her. Her face was glowing like a little sun, and she touched my arm timidly. Then I took both her hands in mine. My mitts were so big and hers so small that I felt as if I were holding tiny birds.

"Do you really think so, Barney? That we can do anything we set our minds to?" she asked.

I took a deep breath, then jumped off with both feet. "Tater, you got a bridle?"

"A bridle? No, not anymore."

"You go get one tomorrow. Start making it soft."

"Why, Barney?" Her eyes were like stars, then, and I'd gone too far to turn back.

"Because you gotta have a bridle for Don Pedro. I figure he's the same as yours, Tater."

Well, that kid! She jumped up and grabbed me and kissed me, and I got all flustered. Then she ran around and kissed Jake and Joe! Then me again.

Finally, she started running out the door, calling out to me. "I'm going to tell Judd and

Dandy about how I'm going to get Don Pedro! We'll go get the bridle tomorrow, won't we, Barney?"

Suddenly Jim Bob said from right under me it seemed, "Want me to kiss you, too?"

I turned around and saw him leaning against the side of the door to the kitchen, holding a frying pan. He looked real pleased with himself or me, I couldn't tell.

"No, I don't want you to kiss me. I might turn into a frog, seeing as how I'm a handsome prince." Then I walked over and said quietly so Jake and Joe couldn't hear, "What you ought to do is kick me from here to the river! What in the world will we do if we can't find a way to get that horse, Jim Bob?"

"I'm bettin' on you, boy. Never was a horse couldn't be rode, never was a cowboy couldn't be throwed. And you jest *got* to ride this here horse! You jest *got* to, boy!"

I stood there trying to find someone to blame for the mess I was in, and when I'd tried everybody I knew in the role, I tried Barney Buck.

I was a perfect fit for the part!

Why was it that every time I made a fool out of myself, I always managed to do it in public? Why couldn't I do one of my fool tricks in private? Just once!

The very day after I promised Tater she'd get Don Pedro, something happened. Jack

Monroe had been waiting to get back at me ever since the first time we met. When it happened, we were all loafing around out at McDonald's eating quarter pounders after a track meet.

I was sitting at a big table with Jake, Joe, Tater, Dandy, and about five more kids, when Jack and Debra came in. They were on their way to the rodeo over at De Queen, but I was too busy.

"Howdy, cowboy!" Jack said and slapped his hand on my back. I tried not to show how much I hated that and just said, "Hi, Jack, Debra. Going to De Queen?"

"Why, shoot, I reckon!" Jack said. He pulled a couple of chairs around and pushed them up to our table, sort of forcing the others to move back or get squashed. "I thought we'd see you there, Buck. Some good prize money. And some good bucking bulls."

"No, don't think I'll make this one."

"Why, you got to get movin' if you want to make all-around this year, Buck." Jack reached over and took one of the quarter pounders from our tray and gave it to Debra, then took another for himself. "I was countin' on your being there—to give me a little competition."

"Come on, Barney!" Debra said. "It'll be fun."

"Gosh, Debra, I've been to so many rodeos the last two weeks I'm dizzy."

Jack had a funny look in his eye, as if he

were about to spring something. There were about fifty kids from our school scattered around in the place. All of a sudden Jack gave a loud shout that just about scared some of the kids to death.

"Yippee! You guys, listen to this!" He waved his burger around, and everybody in the place was listening. "Now what we have here is a good chance for two local heroes to have a friendly little competition. There's me, and there's Barney Buck there. Now why shouldn't we find out who's number one?"

"Well, I don't think I ever claimed to be any great shakes at bareback riding, Jack. I'm learning. That's all."

"Well, I'm gettin' a little tired of hearing how good you are, Buck. I ain't seen nothing all that great, but I got an offer for you."

All of a sudden I knew that he'd set this up. He'd known we'd be here after the meet, and he'd brought Debra in just to show me up in front of her. I flinched a little inside, because I knew whatever he had for me was going to be a doozie!

"Now, I been hearin' about how you and that broken-down guy calls hisself a cowboy been promisin' to get Tater a horse. Course, the way I hear it, looks like she'll be too old to ride by the time you get the animal. That about right, cowboy?"

I got red around the neck, but only said, "Well, we'd like to get the horse for her. That's true."

"Sure you would! I always said you two was closer than a pair of fleas!" Jack grinned. "Don't blame you a bit. If I didn't have me a girl, why, I'd give you a run for your money." He put his arm around Debra's shoulders and looked at me with a cool grin. "What I'm saying is, I can show you a way to get that horse—if you've got the guts to take it."

I felt Tater grow tense at that, but I only said, "What's your game, Jack?"

"Why, like I say, cowboy, we go up against each other. You win; you get to take the horse."

"Barney!" Tater said, but I broke in at once.

"Take the horse?"

"Well, you'll have to pay for him, but in small monthly payments."

"How can that be?"

Jack said, "You didn't know that old man Dillard is my uncle? Why, he admires me so much he'll do anything I ask! True as the Bible, cowboy. All you have to do is beat me and you can take that horse right then for the little girl there and pay for him just a few bucks a month."

"What if I don't beat you? What do I put up?"

Jack gave a shrug, then said, "Why, cowboy, that's what I'm *tellin'* you! You ain't gonna win no way! I'm givin' you this chance because *I* know all this talk about how you're such a hot rider is a lot of bull!" Then he stopped and laughed, "See, Buck, that's the contest. Not horses—we'll both ride the bulls, and the one of us with the best score he's the winner!"

Well, he had really set me up. If I didn't take the challenge, I was a wimp. If I did take him on, I was sure to lose. There was no way I could beat him, even if I had the nerve to get on a bull.

Everybody was staring at me, and I wanted to say, "No thanks."

But Tater was staring at me with her face pale and she was saying, "Please, Barney," with her lips.

Debra wasn't saying a word, but her face was tense. She was staring at Tater, then at me, then back at Tater.

There wasn't a sound, and then Jake said, "Tell the joker to go chase himself, Barney. Never play another man's game."

"That's what he'll do, all right," Jack said. "I never thought he'd take me up. Come on, sugar."

He got up and Debra followed. When they got to the door, I opened my mouth and put my foot in it. "I'll see you at the rodeo next Friday night at Hot Springs, Jack. You just bring the paper with the terms for the horse. I think I'm going to rub your nose in it!"

"Swell! We'll get the whole school there, won't we, sugar?" He pulled Debra out the door. Then she turned and gave me a real strange look as if she were sorry about something.

But nobody was as sorry as I was! Tater was saying, "You'll win! I know you will!"

But she didn't have to get on a ton of bad humor with horns like swords.

It was up to me to do that bit of fast maneuvering!

NINE
The Fool-killer

After they heard about the match between Jack Monroe and me, people just couldn't wait to tell me I was a fool!

Jim Bob took one look at me when I told him about the bet and said, "You're a fool, boy!"

"What! Why, *you* were the one who got me into all this!"

"I never told you to ride no bull. I never told you to play another man's game."

"But we have to get that horse. . . ."

"Sure, but you ain't ready to ride a bull."

"But I already did!"

"For about three seconds!"

"So what? That proved I'm not afraid of bulls."

"Naw, it don't prove that at all. Lots of times when I was fightin' my natural inclination to steer clear of bulldoggin' cows, I'd get over it for a little while! But it'd come back stronger then!"

I stared at him. He stared back, and finally I said, "Well, isn't *this* a pretty come-off! Here I offer to risk my neck to do what *you* want to do, and you rake me over the coals for it."

Jim Bob did something then he hadn't done before. He'd always been sort of stiff. I mean, he'd never been much for *touching* people, like putting his arm around them or stuff like that. So when he came over to me and took my arm in his hand, I knew that was the equivalent of anybody else grabbing me and giving me a hard hug!

"Boy, I–I ain't much good at talk. Never was. But I gotta tell you that. . . ." He tried to go on, choked a little, then said, "Well, I jest don't want you to get hurt—not in no kind of way."

"Oh, Jim Bob. I might get skinned up a little. . . ."

"And you could get crippled for life. But you could get hurt inside. Like if a feller gets scared *real* bad. It's worse than a broken leg. I know lots of cowboys who quit because they got scared so bad they wasn't able to go on."

"You think that could happen to me?"

"Can happen to anybody. So you can still back out of this."

"No," I said slowly. "No, I can't do that, Jim Bob."

He stared at me, then gave me a slow sad smile. "No, I didn't reckon you would. Well, we got to do some talking about this, boy."

He tried to pour all his years of experience into me, but we both knew that I was soaking up only a few fragments. Most of it would fly out of my head when I got on the bull.

Chief Tanner stopped by to talk to me. "You're acting crazy, Barney." Those were his opening words. He went on to explain that he was one of my guardians until Coach and Miss Jean got married and that he didn't think he could allow me to do such a fool thing.

"You want me to quit? To let Tater down?"

Chief squirmed around and tried to find a better way to put it, but couldn't. "Well, I might have known I was wasting my time. You ain't never quit on nothing yet, far as I know. Well, don't get yourself killed on that critter, Barney."

Coach Littlejohn didn't call me a fool, but he was disappointed in me. "Look, Barney, I've already heard from I don't know how many people about this bet you have with Jack Monroe. You have to call it off."

"Why, Coach?"

"Well, aside from the fact that Jean and I are afraid you'll break your neck, it's wrong to gamble. You must know that."

"But, this isn't gambling—exactly."

"Why not?"

"Well, I don't really stand to lose anything, Coach. I mean, I'm not putting up any money or anything like that. And I really don't actually win anything either. I mean, we just get to buy the horse on payment, that's all."

He stared at me with those deep-set gray eyes of his, and I saw why the football players hated to see him coming. He looked real *stern*. "I guess you have a point, but I'm asking you to call it off. Will you do it?"

It was really the first thing Coach had ever asked me to do, but I said, "Coach, if it were just me, I'd do it. But I'm committed to helping Tater get that horse. I think it's more than just a horse to her. You know how she's been shoved around. Well, I think if we can get her this horse, she'll be able to handle things. I guess I'm trying to do what you've always told me to do."

"Which is?"

" 'Do unto others as you would have them do unto you.' "

He gritted his teeth, then slowly let a grin slide over his lips. "Pretty sharp, Buck, quoting Scripture at your poor old dad!"

It always made me feel good when he said something about being my dad, and I could tell he was really proud of me even if he didn't like the bet.

Jake thought I was a sucker. That's the way he put it. "You're a sucker, Barney!"

Joe was nicer, but he said, "Barney, don't do it. You could get killed!"

Mrs. Simpkins told me that I should pick out what clothes I wanted to be buried in, and also she wanted to help me write my obituary for *The Daily Mistake*, our local newspaper.

All in all, it was a pretty bad scene. No light at the end of the tunnel except one, and I was pretty sure that light was from an oncoming train!

"Barney, I don't want you to ride that bull." Debra found me out on the practice field at school watching the marching band practice. Not that I cared much about marching bands, but I wanted to get away and think.

She'd caught me off guard, because they were playing "Stars and Stripes Forever" so loudly I didn't hear her come up behind me. When she touched my arm, I nearly jumped through the goalposts!

"What! Oh, Debra, it's you. You really scared me!"

She sat down beside me and said, "We never talk anymore, Barney."

"Well, you've been so busy with your riding, and I have lots to do."

"I want to. . . ."

"Hey, you won first in De Queen, Debra! That's really great!"

"Well, it's mostly the horse, you know."

"That's not so. Jim Bob says the horse is only half the team. He says you're going to be a champion!"

"Did he really say that?" She smiled and

looked like her old self, and all of a sudden it
made me realize how much I missed the good
times we'd always had together.

"Gosh, Debra, wasn't life simple when we
were younger?"

She burst out laughing and said, "You
sound like my dad. 'Why, when *I* was a boy,
we had to walk ten miles to school! And
through two feet of snow!' " She mocked him
so well I had to laugh.

We laughed together, and I said, "From
what I hear, they must have lived in a
perpetual blizzard in those days."

She giggled, then got serious. She traced the
pattern on my shirt sleeve, and that sent a
few shivers up and down my spine, which
she had a knack for doing. "Barney, will you
do me a favor?"

"If I can. You know that."

"Well, I don't want you to ride the bull at
Hot Springs."

I stared at her. "You afraid I'll beat your
boyfriend?"

I had a way with words. Debra flared up,
but then she shook her head. "No, it's not
that. Jack isn't really interested in me. He
just comes to me to give you a fit."

I was surprised at Debra. I didn't know a
girl could be so smart. I knew that about
Jack, but I didn't think she did! "Well, shoot,
that must make you feel real great!"

"Oh, Jack's been a help. He really does
know horses, and he's given me some good

pointers, but he's in love with somebody else."

"What? With who?"

"Shouldn't it be *with whom?*" Debra giggled and I laughed, too. I was always correcting her grammar, and it tickled her to catch me off guard.

"All right, then, with *whom?*"

"Why, with Jack Monroe, of course. You must have seen that."

"Yeah, but I didn't think you did!"

She pinched me, then got serious. "He's not risking a thing, Barney. But you are. You can get hurt and you can look bad. What can Jack lose?"

"He can lose a lot—if I beat him."

"I wish you could, but he's *real* good, Barney. You know that. If you had a year to practice, it might be different."

"Well, I'm going to do it, Debra. I'm not about to let this chance slip by. You won't be mad at me if I don't do you the favor, will you?"

She smiled at me and pushed my hair back out of my eyes. "No, but you know what I wish?"

"What?"

She leaned closer and whispered, "I wish you were riding that old bull for *me*—not for Tater!"

Then she jumped up and was off.

Well, it was unanimous. I was as nutty as a

pecan orchard for planning to crawl on that bull. But could I do it?

I don't know how it happened, but somebody got our principal to send the school buses to Hot Springs for the rodeo. Usually there had to be something like the end of the world or another flood to get him to do anything like that, but when the rodeo started, almost the entire student body of Cedarville High School was sitting in the stands.

I stared up and Jim Bob grinned at me. He was getting my rig ready for the bareback riding event. "You got lots of friends out there, boy. That ought to make you ride good!"

"What about this horse, Jim Bob? You hear anything about him?"

"Yep. He's a good one."

That meant he was mean and hard to handle. "You want to tell me how to ride him?"

Jim Bob slapped me on the rump as I got up over the animal. "Stay on top of him for eight seconds, boy. That's a good way to start."

Well, I did just that. When the chute opened, the horse, who was named Sweet Dreams by some practical joker, broke out and just about broke in two!

Jim Bob had been right about riding. It was all balance—something I seemed to have. I was letting him snap me forward and back, but I always touched my spurs to his neck and kept my arm held out, pumping back and forth in rhythm to his movements. As always, when I was making a good ride, it seemed to go on forever, and I was caught off guard by the buzzer.

"Great ride!" the pickup man shouted. When he dropped me on the ground, I ducked behind the fence and watched Jack ride. He did better than I ever saw him; I knew I'd been beaten, but that wasn't too much of a bother.

What was giving me a problem was the bulls. They were all bunched up in the corral, and after the calf-roping, they were herded into the chute, six of them. I wandered over to chute number five and found Jim Bob staring down at the bull whose name was Tombstone.

"What do you think, Jim Bob?"

"Well, I dunno, boy. From what I hear, he's a good bull. Plenty of steam, but not bad to go for his man. I think maybe you can do it. You think so?"

It was sort of a bad time. I walked around and peered through the rails, and he looked like all the rest—like bad trouble.

I was relieved that Jim Bob thought I could ride it. I wasn't going to chicken out. Oh, I was *nervous*, but I could handle that. "Well, there never was a bull couldn't be rode."

"I hate to mention it at this particular

130

time," Jim Bob said with a grin, "but that little bit of poetry ain't got no basis in fact. I can name you ten or eleven right off that was never rode."

I stared at him. "You picked a fine time to mention it!"

"Oh, boy, this ain't one of them. He can be had."

We settled back and watched the first contestant, then the next. They hardly got out of the door before they hit the dirt.

Jack was number three, and he didn't do a lot better. He managed to stick on for about four seconds before falling off. He hit the ground rolling, though, and made it out. His face was a little strained as he came to stand by me and said, "Well, I say you came on a good night. That's the sorriest ride I've made all year!"

"Too bad," Jim Bob said. "If you'd taken up that slack like I told you to, you'd still be up there."

Jack sneered. "Let's see how long your little boy stays up there, Bo!"

Then it was my time. I got up on top and Jim Bob was right there. He slid the rigging on so smoothly Tombstone never knew it, and then I was sliding down. There was that moment when I felt those massive muscles tense under me. Two thousand pounds!

Jim Bob said, "Don't fall off on your left, boy. Go to your right!"

Then the world went crazy as the door

slammed open and out went Tombstone! He was like a huge corkscrew, spinning around so fast that the ground blurred in front of my eyes. I felt I was on a gigantic roller coaster with my head reeling and spinning. At the same time my head was popping back and forth so hard I thought my neck would break!

I felt myself going and knew that I couldn't ride until the buzzer sounded; so I started leaning to my right. It should have worked— only it didn't!

Just as I started to slide off on his right, Tombstone shifted, throwing his huge body in a counter spin. I was popped to his left, and all of a sudden I felt myself flying into space!

But my right hand was trapped in the rigging! It was the one thing my mind could remember. The one thing everyone had said to be sure and not do was happening.

The world seemed to go into slow motion. The smell of dust was so strong it choked me. Then I felt myself pulled full length, stopped by the trapped hand. I tried to shake free, but no use. Then it started. Tombstone must have know I was trapped, because he kept throwing those massive horns to his left where I was being dragged, sometimes hitting the ground, sometimes being tossed into the air like a fish trapped on a line.

I thought I saw the clown running up to wave his blanket at Tombstone, but the bull paid no attention. Then suddenly I shook loose and fell onto the ground, right on my back, with every bit of my breath knocked out!

I saw Tombstone whirl like a huge cat, and there was an angry light in his red eyes I'd never seen in a bull. I heard the ground shake as his hooves struck by my head, and all I could see was his massive body over me like a huge tent. I tried to roll over, but couldn't even move my legs. A sharp horn went right between my arm and my body ripping the cloth like tissue paper, and then the fear came.

I lay there watching Tombstone whirl around getting ready to come at me. My throat was burning and every nerve in me was trembling like a tree in a storm.

I'd been scared lots of times, but never had I felt anything like this! It was so bad that I wanted to die so that I wouldn't have to feel it anymore.

Then, it was over—just like that.

The clown got Tombstone's attention, and off he went catching the corner of a huge back pocket in the clown's pants and ripping it. Then someone was picking me up and getting me over the fence.

I was back over the fence and they were saying, "Don't let him move. Get a doctor!"

But I knew that nothing was broken— nothing a doctor could fix, at least.

"I'm all right. Let me stand up!" I said.

Jim Bob was there. "He didn't get you, did he, boy?"

"No." Right then we heard my score, and Jack stepped up and said, "Here's the paper. It says how much you got to pay every month."

Then Tater was hugging me and saying, "You did it! You did it, Barney!"

But it had cost me more than the price of the horse Tater wanted.

Because I knew that no way would I ever be able to force myself to get on another bull!

I knew I was a coward, and that nothing in this world would ever be able to change that.

So we went home with people cheering me, but I wasn't cheering—not at all.

TEN
The Krazy
Kite Kontest

I might have known that Jack Monroe
wouldn't give us a square deal. When we read
the fine print, we found out that we had only
three months to pay for Don Pedro. If we
missed a payment, the horse went back.

"Don't worry, Barney," Tater laughed,
stroking Don Pedro's silky mane. "God
wouldn't let me lose Don Pedro!"

Since I'd been telling her how God was
always ready to take care of us, I couldn't
argue with her, but I worried a lot.

We plugged along, with Jim Bob training
Don Pedro and teaching Tater how to ride.
They both looked so happy, and I thought
Jim Bob was maybe getting better, although
he didn't eat much and he still looked as if he
hurt at times.

I knew we just *had* to keep Don Pedro! I

made some money riding the first month, but travel and entrance fees ate most of it up. When the first payment of $350 was due, we didn't have a dime of it.

I talked about it to Jake and Joe, giving them the whole picture. "So we have to get some money," I finally said.

Jake stared at me. "Are you telling me that you want some help with it, Barney? I mean, you've said some pretty nasty things about my promotions!"

"I know! I know! It just shows you how desperate I am, asking you to dream up something. But try, will you?"

Three days later I was rewarded. Joe met me at the door and said, "Barney, Jake and I have a plan to save Don Pedro."

I stiffened my back and said, "Well, Joe, I asked for it, didn't I? Lead me to it!"

"Come on," Joe said with a big smile on his face. He led me to his workshop, and when we got inside, Jake was standing there with a big grin on his face. "Fifty percent—that's all we ask!" he said right off.

I was staring at the huge affair that took up all the room in the old barn. "Fifty percent of *what?*" I asked. It was pretty dark in the workshop, which was lighted by several sixty-watt bulbs strung from the rafters. What I saw looked like a huge bat, a sort of triangular, flat thing lying on the floor. "What is it?" I asked finally.

"Look at this, Barney," Jake said, shoving a

newspaper under my nose.

I read *"ENTER THE KRAZY KITE KONTEST!!!"* in big letters at the top. Then as I started to read the fine print, Jake snatched the paper away.

"You can read it later, Barney," he said. "What it says is that they're having this kite contest Saturday in Little Rock, and there are cash prizes for all kinds of stuff—the smallest kite, the biggest kite, the highest-flying kite, and the Grand Prize is for. . . ." He paused to read it out loud. " 'The most unusual and imaginative kite which performs the most unusual feat.' "

"And this is it?" I asked. "What does it do that's so unusual?"

Jake cleared his throat and began explaining. "It's got to be really *unusual* to win the Grand Prize. . . ."

"Never mind the pitch," I said. "Just tell me what it does."

"Well, it's like this. . . ."

"It flies *you*, Barney!" Joe said in an excited voice. "See, here's the harness. We just get the Eagle up in the air, and you're sitting here, see?"

"The Eagle?" I asked as I looked at the leather straps that held a sort of seat against the bottom of the kite.

"That's what we call it—the Eagle," Jake said. "What do you think, Barney? Is this a kite or isn't it!"

"And I get on this little seat—have I got

that right?—and then you send the kite up. How far? Oh, that high, eh? And I just glide around up there enjoying the view."

"Oh, that's just part of it, Barney," Joe said. "Look at this!" He shoved something into my hand and said, "It's a two-way radio. See, while you're up there, you do a live *broadcast!*"

I was getting hooked, as always. "So I do this broadcast while I'm up in the Eagle?"

"Right!" Jake beamed. "I got this buddy whose dad owns a station in Little Rock, and I called him. It's all set up, Barney. You'll be on the air all over the world!"

I stared at the microphone, trying to think of some reason for not doing it. "What if the kite falls?"

"Oh, it won't fall." Joe nodded eagerly. "It's like a big hang glider, though. So if it did fall, you'd just have a nice ride down."

"And I'm the one who gets nervous stepping up on the curb!" I said.

"But it's a cinch to win, Barney!" Joe said anxiously.

I stared at the Eagle and thought about it. "In spite of all that I feel about this, I think you may be right. Nobody but you two could come up with such a nutty thing. So we'll do it!"

"Fifty percent!" Jake said quickly. "And that's a bargain!"

"Just so we get enough to make the payment on Don Pedro. You can keep the rest," I said. "When can we test-fly this thing?"

"No need for that," Jake said with a wave of his hand. "The contest is the day after tomorrow, and we have to make some fittings for the pickup."

"The pickup?"

"Sure, you didn't think we could put a thing like that up with a piece of string, did you, Barney?"

"I've given up thinking, Jake. Everything is in your hands now. I'm just a poor country boy trying to get a horse for a poor girl who'll probably go nuts if she doesn't get it. Since I'll probably get squashed flat as a postage stamp in this mad attempt, perhaps you'd like me to go get one last photograph to have something to remember me by."

Jake laughed. "Why, you'll be fine, Barney. I guarantee it."

"So, it's no deposit, no return, is it, Jake? Do or die—that sort of thing?"

"Barney, you been working too hard," Jake said, giving me a pat on the arm. "Now you run along. Joe and I will take care of everything."

As I turned to leave, Jake said to Joe, "Barney's a good guy, but he needs a little motivation, you see. Not too much drive. You and I will have to give him a push now and then."

I'd seen an old movie about paratroopers in World War II, and I remembered that when they went out the airplane door, one soldier stood nearby. It was his job to shove them out.

Jake had been born for a job like that!

And I'd been born to get shoved out.

It would have been nice if I'd had a parachute, but to Jake that would have been a minor detail. Getting me out the door was the really *big* thing!

If I hadn't been so nervous about going up in the Eagle, the Krazy Kite Kontest would have been fun. It was held on a big field just east of town, and there must have been a couple of thousand people there. Judd and all the Crocketts came when they heard I was going up in the air. In fact, Judd was going to help, according to Jake.

A lot of the contestants were kids with their simple little kites, but lots of grown men were there, and they were serious!

All sorts of kites were there, being touched up by the owners. Tiny ones that flew on thread, some that looked like dragonflies, some like snakes, some like bats. All colors, all sizes, all different.

We'd been there all day, and the Eagle had gotten the lion's share of the attention. There was a television crew on hand, and they didn't get too far away. Jake handled the interview, explaining in his important way how the Eagle had been designed. He gave Joe full credit, and I was glad of that. The people at home would get a real kick out of seeing us on the evening news.

The girl with the straw hair and too red mouth finally got to me. "And you're going to go up in this—thing?" she asked brightly. "How do you feel about that, Mr. Buck?"

"On the whole, I'd rather be in Philadelphia." That was the epitaph written on the gravestone of an old-time comedian, but she didn't get it. "Well, do you have any apprehensions about your—er, *flight?*" she asked. "Have you thought about what happens if you fall?"

"Yes, ma'am. I'll come down." I guess I sounded like a smart aleck, but she was too silly. I was glad when she left.

Finally, it was time, and I walked over to the truck. Judd was handling the truck, but Joe was on the winch we'd mounted on the back to hold the Eagle.

"Still time to back out, Barney," Judd said. "I wouldn't get in that thing for a million bucks."

"Don't talk like that, Judd!" Joe said. "It'll be all right. Are you ready, Barney?"

"Why not?" I said with a hollow feeling in my stomach. I walked back to where the Eagle was lying on the ground and looked at the little seat that was attached by a set of nylon cords. I was supposed to strap myself into the seat; then Jake and Joe would take one wing tip apiece. Judd would start pulling the kite along by means of the strong nylon cord that was tied to the nose and fastened to the winch. I would run along, Jake and Joe would keep the tips clear, and up I'd go into the wild blue yonder.

The fact that we'd never actually *done* it didn't seem to bother anybody.

Except me.

Well, Jake gave the signal, I started trotting along, and Judd did a good job of taking the slack out. The breeze caught the big kite, and all of a sudden my feet left the ground!

I'd expected it to go up slowly, but Judd gunned the engine just as Joe piled onto the bed of the pickup. He released the catch, and as the line played out and Judd picked up speed, I went soaring up like a huge bird!

The ground fell away, and Joe on the back of the truck got smaller and smaller. I went up and up and up as if I'd never stop. My feet were dangling, and I gripped the sides of the frail little seat built mostly out of a lawn chair. The microphone was strapped around my neck, but I wasn't thinking about that. I was thinking about how everyone looked like ants.

Well, to tell the truth, at first I was so scared I couldn't even think! But then, it wasn't so bad and even turned out to be *fun!*

Judd had locked the truck into position, and Joe was sitting at the winch, but the wind was really blowing up where I was! It caught at the Eagle, and I have to say that

Joe had done a great job! Why, that kite swooped up and around. It dipped and climbed like a chimney swift, and you can't find a better flier than that bird!

I was having the time of my life when all of a sudden, the two-way phone on my chest buzzed and just about scared me blue. I unclipped the microphone and pressed the little button as Joe had told me. "Eagle here! Come in, Planet Earth!" I thought that was pretty cool! Just like an astronaut!

"Planet Earth, to Eagle!" Jake shot right back. "We read you loud and clear! Proceed with broadcast as planned!"

"Greetings to all of you from Eagle," I said. "I'm watching the beautiful Arkansas River as it curls around the city of Little Rock, a shining silver ribbon that fades away into the western hills. And what a beautiful sight— the skyline of the city, those structures of steel and glass as they point like fingers toward the blue of heaven. I call your attention, ladies and gentlemen, to the newest building on the skyline of our capital city— the Veteran's Hospital—truly a work of art!"

Well, I guess I got carried away with it all. Mr. Burton, our funky English teacher, said I got carried away into what he calls "Purple Prose," but I did get a kick out of stretching words out.

I talked for about fifteen minutes, then started to run dry. "Eagle to Planet Earth. I am ready for reentry. Do you read me?"

"Roger. We read you, Eagle. We will start your countdown."

"Well, sir, I guess Old Jake came up with a good one this time!" I said with a laugh. "Really sort of a shame I have to go down. . . ."

At that moment there was a sudden jerk, and the Eagle rose about two hundred feet almost straight up. Then just as unexpectedly it came to an abrupt halt and shuddered as it hit the end of the cable. "Jake! Jake! What's going on!" I screamed.

"The winch slipped!" I heard Joe say.

"Get me down!" I hollered at the top of my lungs.

I waited for a long time, at least it seemed long, and finally Joe said, "Barney, can you hear me?"

"Get me down from here, Joe!"

"Sure, but it's like this. The winch just slipped and all the line ran out. There's a knot in the end of the line, and that's all that's holding. If I try to pull you back, well, the line may take up, but it could slip out."

"Don't let me go!" I begged.

"We're going to try to clip another line on, but there's nothing to tie it to, no slack in the line. It'll take us about five minutes. Then we'll *have* to try to pull you in."

I sat there shivering in the breeze as the Eagle bucked and dipped. I knew they were doing their best. "All right. Let me know when we're ready."

"Sure, Barney."

Well, there I was.

I was absolutely sure they'd never get me back with the cable. I don't know why I was so sure, but I was. As for the alternative, no matter what Joe had said about the Eagle being a big hang glider, there were several things wrong with that. In the first place, it was so big that I was pretty sure the wind would tip it over. In the second place, I wasn't a hang glider pilot, and in the third place there were no controls.

Which was a rather nasty mess!

I sat there for a few minutes thinking about all the things I should have said to people—things that I'd felt but had been too embarrassed to say.

Now it was too late. Or was it?

The radio! I picked up the microphone and said, "Joe! Joe! Can you hear me?"

Then Joe said, "Sure, Barney."

"Can you record something for me if I talk into the mike?"

Joe mumbled something to somebody on the ground, then said, "Talk on, Barney. We'll record it."

Well, it was hard, but I was pretty sure that I was going to be flat as a plate in not too long a time. I began talking about Coach Littlejohn and told how much I trusted him and how great it had been to have him as a friend. "And you tell Miss Jean that if I had been able to have her for a mom, why, there wouldn't have been anything on earth that would have made me more happy!"

I told how much I thought of Chief and Judd and Mrs. Simpkins and all my buddies at school. Then I told Jake and Joe how much I loved them and how a guy couldn't want brothers any better!

It was real strange, sitting there way up in the clouds all alone saying things I'd been too embarrassed to say face to face. I sort of forgot about being high up, I was so anxious to get it all said.

"Debra, I know we've had our ups and downs," I said, "but you've been my best friend for a long time. You've been so super! And a million times I've wanted to tell you how much you mean to me, but I–I just couldn't do it. But now, just in case I—well, no matter what, I want to tell you this. I love you, Debra!"

That was all.

Joe said, "Barney, we got to try. Are you ready?"

"Sure I am, Joe."

"Barney, are you scared?"

"Joe, I'm going to be riding on the wings of an Eagle, just like that verse we read in the Bible last week. Let it go!"

There was a sudden jerk, and then the Eagle gave a sickening lurch to the side. I knew the cable had slipped!

I was falling then, but not as I had been

dreading. I'd thought that the Eagle would get blown like a piece of paper in the high wind, but it was gliding down in a straight line!

It moved from side to side and took a few dips that made my stomach roll over. As I hung to the sides of my chair, though, I saw that the ground was coming up slowly enough so that with luck I might do no worse than break a leg or two!

The Eagle dipped and made a sharp turn to my left where there were big fields all around. I was glad I wasn't going to land in downtown Little Rock! That would have been a rough landing!

The wind was whistling in my ears and pasting my hair back, and I could see a herd of cattle drinking at a big pond and beyond that some big barns. I hoped I missed them!

Down—down—down! And then it was clear that I wasn't going to crash into a building. There was a small lake or pond dead ahead, and I hoped I'd hit that, because I was coming down pretty fast. I could see a lot of pigs rooting around and beyond them a set of fences that circled a field where they were probably kept at night.

I must have missed the pond by about twenty feet. I came swooping in and hit a muddy section of the field and went down on my face as the Eagle settled down like some huge bird!

I went skidding through the mud, and it smelled like pigs all right! I was back on Planet Earth and covered from head to toe with mud and smelling like a pig, but I'd come home again!

I guess they'd tracked my fall, because the first vehicle I saw was my old pickup with Judd and Debra in the front seat and Joe and Jake bouncing in the bed.

They skidded to a stop, and all of them piled out and just about ate me alive! Why, I never thought there could be such hugging as that.

Then finally Joe said, "Barney! You're famous!"

"For falling like a wet dishrag?"

"No, for the speech you made!" Jake said. "The reporters are all talking about it. It's gonna be on all over the world."

"What! Why, they can't do that! That was *personal!*"

Debra put her arms around my neck, getting mud all over her white dress, and said in that husky voice she got, "Barney, will you say it again—what you said to me up there?"

I was suddenly struck dumb when I remembered what I'd said to her! And now everybody in the whole wide world would hear it and a lot of other things. I gaped like a fish, but I couldn't say one word.

Then that crazy girl laughed and pulled my head down. "Never mind," she whispered.

"You don't have to say it, Barney. After all," she breathed into my ear, "I've got it on a record now, don't I?"

Oh, me!

ELEVEN
Jumping the Fence

"Talk about the skin of your teeth!" I said staring at the figures on the tablet. "With the prize money from the Krazy Kite Kontest, we have just enough to make the payment on Don Pedro!"

We were sitting around the kitchen table—Jake, Joe, Debra, Tater, and I—the Monday after the contest. It was great to have Debra back, just like old times.

Tater had come over as usual, but she was very quiet. I looked at her and said, "Hey, it's *great*, isn't it? I mean, we're on the way."

"Sure, I guess so," she said, then got up. "I have to get home now."

"But—you just got here!"

"Yeah, well, I have some stuff to do. See you later."

After she left, I said, "Gee, I thought she'd

be bubbling over after we got the prize money. She'd have lost Don Pedro if we hadn't!"

Debra looked at me with a worried look on her face. "I guess she figures even if she gets to keep the horse, she's lost something."

"Lost something?" I echoed.

"Barney, don't be *dense!*" she snapped and bit her lip. "Even you ought to know she's had the world's greatest crush on you."

"Yeah, and you sure iced *that* down with that syrupy speech you gave the world from the Eagle!" Jake could be the most obnoxious human being on the planet when he tried. Sometimes when he *didn't* try.

"Oh, she's just a kid, Jake!" I said, remembering what I'd said on that live broadcast. Just thinking about it made me turn red as a traffic light.

"Well, shoot, Debra!" I said. "You've offered to help her with her riding. I think that's pretty good for Tater!"

She patted my hand and gave me a smile that made me feel like a kid. "But *I'm* not what she wants, Barney. *You* are!"

Why is it that every time something good happens, something bad has to come along? It was really great to get back with Debra, but she was right about Tater. I wasn't a movie star or anything like that, but it was pretty obvious that Tater did like me. Judd said when she heard what I'd said about Debra over the radio, she got white as a sheet, then ran off, and cried all night long!

I tried to make it right, of course, but it was no good. She stayed away from our place and whenever I went to the Crocketts, she always managed to be too busy to talk to me.

It was the same way at school. She'd been sticking to me like a postage stamp for a long time, but now she started spending a lot of time with some other kids—mostly those who were into riding horses and were pretty wild. Dandy and I talked about it, but she said Tater would just have to find out for herself who her friends were. Judd said about the same thing; so I talked to Jim Bob about it.

I found him lying down on the couch with his eyes closed although it was early afternoon. That worried me a little bit, because he'd started doing that pretty often. He wasn't eating much, and I'd tried to get him to go see Doctor Rogers, but he wouldn't.

"You asleep, Jim Bob?"

He jumped a little and his eyes flew open. "Asleep! Heck, no, boy. Jest thinking about that next ride of yours." He slowly pulled himself up and rubbed his right arm with his left hand.

"You been doing that a lot," I said. "Does it hurt?"

"What? Oh, shoot no, boy! Jest went to sleep on me. What's happening?"

"Well, I'm worried about Tater. She's mad at me, and she's getting in with a pretty fast bunch."

He nodded slowly, and I noticed again how pale his face was. "Yeah, I know. But you don't go blaming yourself. You've done a heap for that girl. She's jest mixed up."

"We got to do *something*, Jim Bob. I mean what will happen to her if she loses that horse?"

"I dunno, boy. I jest dunno." He rubbed his arm again, and I made up my mind to talk to Coach about it. "It's times like this that make me wish I'd lived my life different. Old and broke! Can't help nobody!"

I opened my mouth to say what I'd been trying to say to Jim Bob for a long time— that he needed Christ in his life.

But I didn't. It just couldn't come out. I always had trouble talking about the Lord to people, and I knew that I had to get some help.

I drove over to Coach Littlejohn's apartment and pinned him down.

"Coach, I'm worried about Jim Bob." I told him about how weak the old man was getting and all the symptoms I'd noticed.

"I don't know, Barney," he said after he thought it over. "He's got to go see a doctor."

I snorted, "It'd take a tractor to drag him in, Coach. I've tried! But I'm going to outfox him. I'm going to get Doctor Rogers to come to the house. Get him trapped, you see. But there's another thing, and that's what I came to ask you." I took a deep breath and told him that Jim Bob didn't know God and needed to be told. "So I think you ought to go tell him, Coach."

He gave me a long look, then shook his head. "Nope. I'm not the one, Barney. You're the one God's put in that place to help the man. You picked him up and you know him. I'd say you've been the best friend he's maybe ever had. So I think you're the evangelist to win Jim Bob to the Lord."

"Me! I'm no evangelist!"

"Sure you are." He grinned. "You think all evangelists go around with tents and loudspeakers? No, Barney, an evangelist is basically one who brings good news. So you give the good news to Jim Bob."

He wouldn't budge, and I left dreading the time I'd have to talk to Jim Bob about becoming a Christian.

If it hadn't been for Jim Bob, I would have stopped riding in the rodeos. Not that I didn't like the bronc riding, but Jack Monroe had taken all the fun out of it.

Debra met me one morning before school. "Have you seen Jack?" she said nervously.

"Jack? No, not this morning."

"Barney, you have to watch out for him." She took my arm and said in a trembling voice, "He came over to my house yesterday, and we had a fight."

"About what?"

"Well, about you! He kept saying mean things about your being afraid of bulls, and finally I told him to leave and not come back."

"What did he say?"

"He just laughed! He couldn't believe any girl could say no to him. Then, when he saw I meant it, he looked real mean. He said he'd get you."

"Just talk, I guess."

"No." Debra shook her head. "He meant it, Barney. You stay away from him."

Well, that wasn't so easy. We were in the same school and went to the same rodeos. He never mentioned Debra at all, but he never missed a chance to needle me about being afraid of bulls.

I put up with it, though, and after a couple of weeks, I thought he'd had enough of it.

But I was wrong.

I was cleaning my Browning Sweet Sixteen one night when I heard a car pull up to the house. "Pretty late for company," I said to Jim Bob. "Must be nearly ten o'clock."

We got up, and when I opened the door, Judd Crockett came in. He had a frown on his face. "Has Tater been over here?" he said in a worried voice.

"Tater? Why, no, Judd. I haven't seen her since school let out today."

"What's wrong, Judd?" Jim Bob asked.

"Well, I don't know for sure, but I'm worried. Tater went over to spend the night with Millie Bryant. She does that a lot lately.

155

But Mr. Bryant called me and said she'd slipped off with some guy."

"He say who it was?" Jim Bob asked.

"Said it looked like that souped-up Trans Am Jack Monroe drives."

"That one? That gal snuck off with *him?* I thought she knowed better."

"I–I think it's my fault," I muttered. They stared at me and I went on. "Debra ran Jack off, and he said he'd get even with me. I didn't think he'd do it this way, though!"

Judd's eyes got narrow, and I remembered that he'd led a pretty wild life up until a year ago. Now he was like a bomb set to go off.

I grabbed him as he turned and started for the door. "Where you going?"

"Gonna find her!"

"You don't know where they are, do you?" I asked.

"I figure if I check enough rat holes, I'll flush the sucker out!"

I picked up my jacket and said, "Jim Bob, you tell the boys where I've gone."

"Leave 'em a note, boy. Think *I'm* gonna stay home?" He was pulling on his frayed old jacket, and his hands were trembling. I took one look at his set face and knew it would be a waste of time to argue.

"Come on if you're coming!" Judd said, and we all went out and piled into his car.

I guess if it hadn't been for that part of Judd's life when he had been running around, drinking, and getting into all kinds of trouble, we'd never have found Tater that night. He made a stop at a place just outside of town with all the windows painted black. When he came out, he said, "I think I got a line on them," and drove us to Hot Springs.

He stopped at one place outside of Hot Springs with a parking lot full of cars and music that just about split my eardrums. He was in there for about thirty minutes, and I started getting worried. "Maybe I better go in and see what's wrong."

"No, you jest set," Jim Bob grunted. He closed his eyes and put his head back on the seat. "Judd knows how to handle himself in places like that. You don't, thank the Lord."

I shot him a glance. "You really mean that, Jim Bob? Thank the Lord?"

He lifted his head and stared at me with dark circles under his eyes. "You been tryin' to talk to me about God, ain't you, boy?"

"Well, yes. . . ." I stopped and then he gave me a smile.

"Well, I guess you might as well have at it, boy. Turn your wolf loose."

We sat there in the warm darkness, and by the light of the red neon light I watched his face as I told him what Christ had done for me. It was real simple, and when I was through, he was quiet. "Don't you think it's time you gave God a chance, Jim Bob? He loves you."

He didn't move for a minute. Then he

nodded his head, and I saw a silver streak speed down his wrinkled face. "I–I have to say it's past time, boy. But I heard once the Lord takes in even the ole sorry prodigals."

By the time Judd came out, Jim Bob had settled it all, and I don't think I was ever gladder about anything!

But Judd broke into my thoughts when he piled in and said, "I got 'em. They was here, but a guy I know says they're at the Midnight Club." He started the engine and said, "Don't let me kill that feller, you guys. Just bust him up a little!"

The Midnight Club looked like a big box with no windows and another parking lot full of cars and trucks. This time we all got out and went inside. It was so dark I couldn't see a thing, but in a few minutes I began to notice a lot of tables on one side of the room and a long bar on the other. The place was packed, but it took Judd only about two minutes to find them. I guess he was used to dark places like that.

"There they are." He pushed his way through the crowded floor and came to a booth that held Jack and Tater.

Tater looked pitiful! She was all dressed up in a fancy dress and with three times too much makeup. I guess she thought it would make her look older, but she looked about twelve years old.

Jack was caught off guard. He looked up and probably saw that Judd was trouble.

"Hey, look who's here, old Judd—and Barney! Cowboy, I didn't know you came to spots like this! You know Barney Buck the Sunday school kid came to dives, Hartley?"

I didn't know the guy with him, but he looked like a fugitive from the law. He was with another young girl and just glared at us as if he wanted to waste us.

"Come on, Tater," Judd said, real tight-lipped. "Let's get out of here."

Tater looked at me, then shook her head. "I'm not going, Judd."

Jack and the other guy slipped out of the booth. "Judd, you're out of your class. Take the kid and the old man out of here before you get hurt."

Judd stared at him. "Jack, if you don't sit down and shut up, I'm gonna put you in traction for about two weeks."

Judd was slim and not too tall, while Jack was big and strong as a bull. But something about the way Judd spoke made Jack take a second look. He might have backed off, but the other guy named Hartley took over. He gave Judd a shove that drove him back against Jim Bob, saying, "You punks get outta here."

Then everything went wild. Judd wasn't big, but he was fast as a cat! I saw him lean forward, and his hands blurred as he hit Hartley about four times. It made a loud slapping noise, and Hartley went down with a crash into a nearby table. Suddenly Jack turned and hit *me!* I saw all kinds of flashing lights and landed flat on my back.

It took me a minute to focus my eyes. When I got up, Hartley and Jack were pinning Judd against the wall and hitting him with big swinging blows.

I'd never hit anybody since I'd been in the third grade, but I knew I had to do something!

I really didn't have time, and while I was trying to get my mind made up, Jim Bob picked up a chair and hit Hartley over the head. Hartley slumped to the floor. Jack stared at him, and Jim Bob picked up a heavy bottle that had a candle in it and said, "You want your head split or unsplit, joker?"

Jack took a step backward, and Judd came to stand beside us. He reached down and pulled Tater to her feet. Her face was like paste and her mouth was open. She didn't say a word, but started for the door with Judd.

Jim Bob tossed the bottle down and followed. Then Jack said, "You won't always have somebody around to do your fighting for you, Buck. You'll wish you never saw me before this is over."

"I already wish it, Jack," I said.

Then I left and got into the back seat of the car. Tater was crying in the front with Judd, and Jim Bob was leaning back.

We pulled out of the lot and started for home, but before we'd gone too far, Jim Bob turned his head toward me. "Boy?"

"Yes, Jim Bob?"

He laughed softly and said, "Seems funny to me."

"What does, Jim Bob?"

"Why, don't you see? Here I am a Christian for five minutes and already in a barroom fight!" He smiled. "You think that cancelled me out?"

I put my arm around him and gave him a hard squeeze—something I wouldn't have done before.

"No, I think you did what the Lord wants us all to do—help those we can. But I'm hoping it won't always be by breaking a chair over somebody's head!"

Tater was really pretty glad to see us. Anyway, that's what she told Dandy after she got home. She had been scared to death and didn't know how to get out of it.

The next day she met me in the hall and turned red as an apple, but she came right up to me and said, "Barney, I–I'm glad you came last night. Thanks."

That was all, but I felt that she was going to be all right.

But then I met Jack out on the parking lot after school, and he handed me a paper. "Let's see who gets the last laugh, cowboy!" he said.

When I read the paper, I almost got sick! He'd found the way to hurt me, and I couldn't do a thing about it.

TWELVE
The Only Way
to Look

"Take Don Pedro!" Jim Bob snorted. "How's he think he can do that? We made the payment, didn't we?"

"Yes, but there was some fine print in that sales contract we didn't read," I said, feeling miserable. "Look here. . . ."

"Jest tell me what it says!"

"Well, it says that the seller has the right to demand the full price of the horse at any time. And he can demand the return of the horse if he's not paid in ten days."

That was what Jack handed me on the parking lot—the sales contract with that clause outlined in red.

"You have that money in ten days, or else I'll be there to pick up the horse!" he'd said with a sneer.

Jim Bob looked pretty sick. I guess I did, too.

"Never could read them lawyer papers," he said.

"We should have had a lawyer look at them, or maybe Chief. But we thought we were getting such a good deal. I *trusted* Jack!"

"No sense cryin' about it. We gotta get that money. How much is it?"

"Close to seven hundred."

"You got any dough at all, boy?"

"No, not a dollar. And Judd doesn't have it either."

Jim Bob thought about it, then said, "We gotta tell Tater. Can't let her find out from that skunk!"

I knew he was right, and we went over to the Crocketts. Judd was gone but Tater was there. She turned red when she saw us. I guessed she was thinking about her escapade with Jack. Then she realized we were there on serious business. "What's wrong?"

"Plenty, I reckon," Jim Bob said. He stood in front of her and put his hands on her shoulders. "You're a Texas gal, and you got to handle what we got to say, all right?"

She stared at him, then at me. "What is it, Jim Bob? It's about Don Pedro, isn't it?"

"Yeah, it is." He gave it to her, and I waited for her to cry.

But she just bit her lip and nodded. She looked at me and said, "I guess I deserve this, after the way I acted."

"No, you don't, Tater," I said. "Jack's doing it to get even with me."

"But we ain't gonna let him get by with it!" Jim Bob suddenly exploded. He drove his fist into his palm. "We just gotta outfox that sucker!"

Tater shook her head. "It would cost too much, Jim Bob. Judd would buy Don Pedro, but it takes all he can bring home just to feed us all. I–I'll just have to give him up."

I was real proud of Tater! She loved that horse more than you could say, but she wasn't falling apart.

Jim Bob hauled off his battered Stetson and clawed his sparse white hair. He looked blank, then suddenly gave me a wide-eyed look. "Boy, I ain't forgot what I done in the car the other night, that I trusted the Lord."

"I know that, Jim Bob."

"Well, I done started reading the Book, the Bible, you know? Started in the first of it, but I got bogged down with all them big names."

"That *is* hard!" I agreed.

"But I went to the other end, and I found out that a lot of it's wrote in red letters."

"Sure, the words of Jesus are printed in red in some Bibles."

"Yeah? Well, I sure do like that red part! And I think maybe I got us something there, what was wrote in red. Lemme see. What was it? Something like, 'Anything you ask the Lord for, you're gonna get it.' You ever read that in the Book?"

"Well, sure, Jim Bob, but it goes on to say you have to ask in faith."

"What's that mean?"

"It just means you have to believe you'll get what you pray for."

He grinned and said, "Shoot, is that all? Well, we got nothing to worry about, then. If the Book says it in the red part, I reckon it's gonna be so, ain't that right?"

Our pastor said once that when somebody gets saved, he has to backslide before he can have fellowship with the rest of the church members. He said we forget the simple things that we start out believing and get too smart for our own good. Jim Bob had me in a bind!

"Well, sure, Jim Bob, but we got to use common sense!"

He stared at me. "Does it say *that* in the Book in red?"

"N–no, but. . . ."

"But nothing! I say let's jest get in the saddle and ride this bronc trustin' the Lord to keep us in the leather!"

"Do you think it'll happen, Barney?" Tater asked.

Why was I such a wimp? I was all the time *saying* I believed the Bible. Why did I dodge around when something like this came up? Finally, I said, "Well, I'll believe it if both of you will. The red part says that if any two of you will agree on anything, it'll be done."

So that was it. They both laughed and I tried to look happy, too. But after they calmed down, I said, "You know, the Lord sometimes wants us to be involved in the answers to prayer. I mean, we can't just sit down and wait. We need to get busy and find out if there's something we can do. Even if it looks impossible, it may be what God wants to use, to keep Don Pedro."

"Oh, I done got that figured out, boy." Jim Bob nodded.

"You have!"

"Sure. Oh, I thought about it a couple of times, but never said nothing, 'cause it seemed too crazy. But now that we're agreed and all, why I think it'd work fine."

"You sound so much like Jake I'm afraid to ask what it is," I said with a grin.

"Why, it ain't nothin' *new*, boy. It's the big state rodeo at Little Rock on the fifteenth. That's the day the note's gotta be paid, ain't it?"

I counted up the days and said, "That's the date, but what's the big plan?"

Jim Bob shook his head. "Boy, you must be extra slow this morning! I mean we ask the Lord to give us the money to pay a bill that's due on the fifteenth and here you've been learnin' to ride for a spell and here's the biggest prize money of the year and what day does it come on? Why, it's plain that the Lord's gonna let you win the all-around at that rodeo!"

I stared at him. "But the best riders in the

country will be there for that one!"

"But they ain't got the part in red workin' for them!" Jim Bob said with a shout. "They jest ain't got nothin' but natural ability. You got the Lord on your side, ain't you, boy?"

I guess it was pretty wild theology, but it was clear to those two that we were going to win. I wasn't so sure.

Jim Bob was counting up on his fingers. "Lemme see now, there's you riding the barrels, Tater, and you on the saddle-bronc competition, boy. You can get Jake to team up with you, and you two can win the wild steer milkin' contest. And you can learn goat throwin' and win that, Tater. And Joe can win the calf-riding event, and you can win the bull riding, boy. . . ."

I felt I'd touched a live wire. I guess Jim Bob must have seen it, because he stopped and said, "Why, what's the matter?"

"Jim Bob, I can't—well, you know I can't ride a bull! Can't even look at one!"

"Why, sure, I know you *used* to have that problem, but that was before we agreed to trust the Lord, wasn't it?"

"Look, I'll do all the rest of it, but not that!"

"You *got* to, boy! We'll need every point we can get! Even third place will be good money in a meet like that one. You gotta do it."

I felt the sweat pop out on my face just thinking about it! Tater said, "No, Jim Bob.

We can't ask Barney to do that!"

The old man stared me right in the eye. "Boy, you got me to believing in the Lord. Now I want you to tell me if that was all just guff! If God can't get you so's you can get on a bull, what good is he gonna do me? Or you, for that matter?"

I stood there trying to think, and my head was swimming! I knew he was being a little too simple about the whole matter of praying. He'd have to learn that God wasn't a Santa Claus dumping out presents right and left. But that would come. Right now, Jim Bob was on the edge. If I didn't agree to ride a bull, he was just likely to throw the whole thing out!

Finally, I said, "Look, all I can say is that right this minute, I couldn't get on a bull. Now, we'll go to the rodeo, and if God gives me the nerve to get on, why I will. If he doesn't, there's no way I can do it. That's all I can promise."

Jim Bob grinned and said, "Boy, that's plum good enough fer me. I know you'll do 'er!"

He may have thought so, but I had doubts enough for both of us!

You know, for all the pressure we had, we had a *great* time for the next few days getting ready to go to Little Rock.

Jake agreed to team with me in the wild steer roping, and we practiced on some of the cows on farms around close. Jake was a good hand at it, and I thought we had a chance.

Joe was happy as a lark learning to ride some of the yearlings, and he had a good chance to win.

Jake had a wild idea or two, of course. He had about twenty a day with gusts up to fifty! One of them was to sneak a little Super Glue onto the seat of my pants so I'd be glued to the horse! He sure hated to give up on that, but I talked him out of it.

Tater was going great on the barrels, and she and Debra worked together. They'd be competing against each other, but you never saw them when they weren't laughing and having fun.

The only thing that spoiled it was Jack. I don't know what I did for trouble until he came to town. He got wind of our plan, and of course he told it in a lopsided way to make us all sound like lunatics!

"You hear about the Bucks and the Crocketts?" he'd say when a crowd was together. "Heard they was going to the State Finals and win every event. Way I hear it, God's gonna just hand them first place 'cause they're so nice and sweet! Not much sense in us ordinary sinners going, I reckon!" He'd get his laugh, and soon the whole town was laughing at us.

Jim Bob heard it all, of course. He asked me once, "I run across something in the red part last night, boy. Said you was supposed to love your enemies."

"Yes. That's pretty hard."

"You do that, boy? You love that Monroe feller?"

"Well, I guess you'd have to say I'm working on it, Jim Bob. Making progress."

"Well, I ain't making much," he growled. "I'd like to have the sucker put to sleep!"

"Yeah, I know. He's a real pain. But I guess we all are at one time or another."

"Yeah, sure. But I'd sure like to punch his face—in a good Christian way, of course!"

"Don't do that," I laughed. "Just try to do what the red part says. He needs the prayer and you need the practice!"

So, it wasn't a bad time getting ready for that big show.

Except for the nights.

Every single night I'd dream that I was being chased by a huge bull with red eyes and horns like telephone poles. And just before he caught me, I'd wake up. But I knew that when I *really* got into the arena with a bull and he started for me, there wouldn't be any waking up from that!

Finally, the day came. We loaded the horses into a double trailer, piled into the pickup and Judd's car, and started for the big arena.

"How do you feel, Barney?" Debra whispered.

I thought about it, then said, "I feel how the Christians must have felt when the lions were turned loose on them. Scared to death!"

It was sixty-five miles from Cedarville to

Little Rock. I left two heel marks all the way there! I tried to be optimistic about it all, but I have to admit that the closer we got, the more I felt like it was Thanksgiving Day and I was the turkey!

THIRTEEN
A Hero's Ride

The finals of the Arkansas High School Rodeo lasted for two days. Barton Coliseum was packed out when we got there, and it looked huge after the little arenas I'd been riding in.

"Jim Bob, I'm scared just *being* here! I won't be able to do a thing!"

He leaned against the wall by the concession stand and took a couple of pills with a swig of Sprite. "Horse is a horse, boy. Don't make no never-mind if it's out in a pasture or in Madison Square Garden with thousands of folks watching. When that chute opens, it's jest you and him."

"Didn't you ever get nervous?"

"Sure, but 'bout the horse, not the folks who was watchin'!" He tossed the empty bottle into a waste can, saying, "Let's go look at the stock."

I knew he was doing it to calm me down,

and I *needed* it! We walked around looking at
the horses, and I recognized quite a few of
the contestants. It's a pretty small world,
after all, more like a club where you run
across the same people over and over.

We'd dropped by to see the bulls, and I
wasn't too surprised to see Jack sitting on a
rail staring at a bull. When he saw us, he got
down with an easy leap and leaned back
against the bar. "Well, well, if it ain't the
famous Barney Buck!" He thumbed his hat
back and drawled, "I almost didn't come,
seein' as how you're goin' to take all the
money home."

Jim Bob said quietly, "Don't act like that,
son. You're a good hand, but you think that
ain't enough. You got to hold the center stage
all the time."

Jack's face burned, and he took a step
toward Jim Bob. "Old man, you stay clear of
me! Maybe you think you can go breaking
chairs on heads and nobody'll call your hand
'cause you're old and wore out. Don't you
believe it! You open your mouth to me, and I'll
put you down, you hear me!"

Jim Bob just smiled. "I hear you. Feel sorry
for you, Jack. You got a rocky road ahead of
you."

"And what you got, old man? Old, sick, and
a charity case! Who are you to be feeling
sorry for anybody?"

"Come on, Jack! Knock it off!" I said.

He whirled and gave me a shove with his

thick hand. "I'll knock it off, all right! Sooner or later I'm gonna take you down! You make me sick!"

He stalked off and I said, "Why does he hate me so much, Jim Bob?"

"I think that boy's afraid he ain't as good as he's supposed to be. Always like that. I hear tell the beauty queens ain't never satisfied with their looks, and the big guys like Jack are so scared they got a little human weakness in 'em, they just try to stomp anything that gets in their way."

"Why, Jack's got everything! He's big, strong, good looking, and he's got lots of money. . . ."

"Boy, you got more man in your little finger than Monroe's got in his whole body!"

"Me! Why, I'm scared even of bulls!"

"You won't be, after you win first money in the bull riding tomorrow." He grinned and said, "I found me that place in the Book and drew a line under it, see?"

He'd hauled a New Testament out of his hip pocket and opened it. A circle had been drawn around Matthew 21:21, 22. He read it out loud, stumbling a little over the words: "If you shall say unto this mountain, be thou cast into the sea, it shall be done. And all things, whatsoever ye shall ask in prayer, believing, ye shall receive." He waved the New Testament around and said, "Well, ain't that *neat!* And it's one of them sayings in red, too!"

He kept on talking until it was time for the show to start, and it wasn't to keep me from getting nervous. Jim Bob was excited about the things in the Bible that I'd gotten excited over when I first found out what a great book it was. It made me promise myself to get back to it.

Well, there we were, a bunch of crazy fools with a wild notion that we were going to win a bunch of prize money over people who were older and had a world more experience.

One good thing. I didn't have to face the bull-riding competition the first night. I had drawn a ride on the following night. "Maybe I'll break my neck riding the bronc. Then I won't have to face the bull!" I muttered to myself. But I knew I couldn't be so lucky.

It would take me a month to tell about that night. About how Joe won second place in the calf riding, and Tater won first on goat roping! Then Jake and I just about got killed in the steer milking contest, but got third-place money!

Both Tater and Debra were scheduled to ride the barrels the following night; so they were back at the chute when it was time for the bareback riding.

I was so glad I didn't have to get on a bull that it was easy to make my ride, even if there were more people watching me than I'd ever seen in one place!

I was the last rider. Jack had made a great ride, but so had about five other contestants.

This was the big time, and as I settled down onto the horse and fitted my hand into the rigging, Jim Bob said softly in my ear, "I'd sure like to make one more ride, boy. I sure would!" Then he gave me a little tap on the top of my hat and said, "Guess you're gonna have to do it for me, boy. Show these birds how it's done!"

Cyclone was the name of my horse, and he about behaved like one! He threw a fit in the stall; then when he did settle down long enough for them to throw the gate open, he came out like a big cat, twisting and hunching like crazy. My head was popping so fast I didn't have time to think about what to do, but all the riding I'd been doing had built some reflexes into me.

I felt Cyclone's huge muscles bunch, and when he uncoiled, I relaxed instead of tensing up, which would have shot me off like a bullet. It was all balance, and even though he bucked so hard my nose started bleeding, I stayed on until the buzzer sounded.

I slid off without waiting for the pickup man and stood there swaying while my head cleared. Then I heard fifty thousand people clapping and hollering, and it was for *me!* I knew then why some sports heroes and actors go on after they get too old!

My score would have been good enough to win almost anywhere else, but I took third. Jack won, and I tried to congratulate him, but he just shoved by me.

We'd done pretty well, and all of us were excited. Tater and Debra gave me a hug at the same time, and that was better than getting stuck in the eye with a sharp stick!

"If I win at the barrels tomorrow, will we have enough to buy Don Pedro?" Tater asked.

"Wait a minute," Debra said. "I'm in that contest, too, Tater."

"Oh, sure, Debra. . . ." Tater nodded.

"Well, if I win any prize money, it goes into the pot," she said. "We Goober Holler folks have got to stick together, don't we?"

Jake had his tablet out and was adding up figures with a stubby pencil. "As I see it, folks, it's in the bag. . . ."

"Hooray!" Joe shouted, and we all started grinning.

"As I was *about* to say . . . ," Jake raised his voice. "We got it made, *if* Barney does at least fair in the bull riding."

Well, that put a damper on me! I had managed to forget that I'd have to face a ride on one of those bulls tomorrow. Now I gulped and cleared my throat. "Actually, I'm feeling pretty weak in the knees about that. No sense kidding you."

Debra gave me a smile. "I'm not worried. Any guy who will say, 'I love you' to a girl on a national broadcast won't be whipped by a little old Brahman!"

I started stammering and blushing. She'd found out that any reference to the "Great Broadcast" did that to me, and I thought it was pretty mean to bring it up. But I knew she was trying to help.

"Looks like it's about time for tonight's bull riding," I finally said. "Jack's riding, and we ought to give him a hand."

"What! That hunk of hokum!" Jake squealed. "I'd like to give him a one-way ticket to the North Pole!"

"Well, let's go watch anyhow." I had a thought. "Let's watch from the lower level. Maybe if I get close to those things tonight, it'll help get me ready for tomorrow."

"Not a bad idea," Jim Bob said with a nod.

We made our way to the area close to the chute, and I saw one of them open. A bull came roaring out just as we got there. The rider stayed on for the full eight seconds, and I relaxed as he got away from the bull.

The rest of them were watching the bulls, but I knew Jim Bob was watching me. He finally leaned in close and said, "Is it pretty bad, boy?"

"Well, pretty bad."

He nodded. "I can tell. If it was any ordinary time, I'd tell you to stay off the animal. But this time we got the good Lord ridin' with you. Besides, I don't want you to go through life bein' scared of anything." Then suddenly he said, "There's Jack. Looks like he's havin' trouble with his bull. Maybe I can help."

"Well, he'll probably just cuss you out."

"Won't hurt none. It's been done before.

Anyway, I found me another saying in red in the Book. Said to 'turn the other cheek.' Come on, boy. You got a cheek or two to turn yourself."

We went over and climbed up on top of the chute, and Jack's bull was fighting like crazy, kicking and banging with his massive horns against the stall.

"Need some help, Jack?" Jim Bob said.

Jack was straddling the chute, his eyes riveted on the plunging bull. He cut his glance around and saw us. "I don't need no help from a washed-up old bum and a coward!" he snapped.

"It's your say, Jack," Jim Bob said, and we stepped back. "You can't mess with a man's bull if he says no."

Finally, the bull got still enough for Jack to get on, and I saw that he was taking an extra turn with the rope around his wrist.

"He'll never get that rope off!" I gasped.

"No, he won't," Jim Bob shook his head. "That's a fool stunt."

Then the gate swung open and out they went.

But it was a mess! I don't think Jack ever got really situated. Just as the bull started to twist one way, it changed direction and snapped Jack off like a rag doll, but something was wrong.

"He's caught, Jim Bob! He can't get loose!"

Everybody saw it, and the clown came running in just as Jack's feet hit the ground.

Ordinarily the clown would have gotten the attention of the bull by flapping a red towel in his face, but this time he never made it.

Just as the clown made his pass with the towel, the bull felt the weight of Jack hanging on, and he ignored the clown and swept around in a half circle, huge horns whistling through the air.

That clown really did his best, and it almost got him killed. He saw that the bull was going for Jack; so he just jumped right up in that animal's face, and got swiped with one of those huge horns! It must have felt like getting hit in the head with a baseball bat. The clown went rolling in the dust and looked practically helpless.

But the bull didn't go for him. He went for Jack!

Jack was still anchored by the rope, and every time he tried to get away, he was whipped back by the short line. He was getting punched by the broadside of the bull's horns and kicked over and over by those slashing legs.

I wanted to jump into the arena and help him, but it was as if my boots were riveted to the ground! My mouth was opening and closing, but it was like the time I was running an electric saw and standing on wet concrete. It had shorted out, and I'd tried to throw the saw away, but all I could do was stand there and shake until Jake pulled the plug and saved my life.

That was how it went, and I knew I'd have nightmares and ask myself a thousand times why I didn't do something!

Then I caught a flash of movement to my right, and suddenly Jim Bob was in the arena, running right for the bull!

He didn't try to get the bull's attention by slapping at him. Instead, he ran right at him, threw both arms open wide and leaped up and grabbed the bull's head with a hammerlock!

He had leaned over the huge head and one horn was under each of his arms and his hands were locked under the bull's throat!

Then that bull went crazy, probably because he was suddenly blind, or maybe because he didn't want anything messing with him.

However it was, he forgot about Jack, who suddenly came loose and fell to the ground unconscious. A couple of hands ran out and pulled him out of the arena, and he flopped like a rag doll as they hauled him out in a hurry.

Up and down went the bull's head, and Jim Bob's fragile body snapped like a whip as he was thrown first high, then smashed against the ground.

I knew nobody could take that kind of punishment long!

Then one of Jim Bob's arms came loose, and he was thrown along the ground as the bull gave a sweep of his head. When he hit the ground, he looked boneless he was so limp!

He rolled right up close to the fence where I stood frozen. His eyes were open, but he was totally unconscious. A thin line of blood trickled from his lips. It was scary seeing him lying there.

Then the bull whirled and made for him, horns lowered like bayonets!

Now was the time for me to be a hero! In the storybooks, I would have leaped into action and saved his life.

But I didn't. I just stood there.

Suddenly Tater jumped into the arena and ran right at the bull!

She looked like a doll next to that monster. Waving her red hat in his face, she pulled him right away from Jim Bob. He made a pass at her, but she was as fast as a hawk! Bobbing and weaving and slapping his nose with her ridiculous hat, she flirted with that killer bull as if he were a woolly lamb!

Well, it didn't last long, of course. Two pickup men darted in, slapping at the bull, and Tater scooted out and dodged between the bars.

I ran to where they had put Jim Bob on the ground, and nearby Jack was just getting to his feet, but not really seeing anything.

I knelt down and cradled Jim Bob's head in my hands, but he was still limp as a dishrag. Tater knelt beside me, crying without making a sound. Then she said, "He'll be all right, won't he, Barney?"

"Course he will!" I said, but when the stretcher men came and I rode in the ambulance to the hospital, Jim Bob never moved. They were giving him shots of some sort, and they put a mask over his face, but he never moved a muscle.

We all stayed out in the hall of the hospital until they herded us into a waiting room. We were there until a doctor came out in about two hours.

He was a tall, thin man with thick glasses, maybe about thirty years old. "Are you Mr. Puckett's family?" he asked.

We looked at each other, and Tater slipped her hand into mine.

"Yes, doctor, we're his family. How is he?"

"He's a very sick man. Aside from the internal injuries, he's got a heart problem, which I guess you knew about."

I looked at him and slowly shook my head. "No, we didn't know. But I'll tell you one thing, doctor, his heart is the biggest thing about Jim Bob Puckett!"

Well, we spent all night in the waiting room. Jim Bob came to about four o'clock and they let me in. He looked so *little* in that bed, and his eyes were closed. I thought for one awful moment he was dead!

Then he slowly opened his eyes and saw me. He gave a ghost of a grin, and said in a whisper so faint I had to lean close to hear it, "Well, boy, I had me one last ride, didn't I?"

"You—you're going to have lots of rides, Jim Bob. You got to get well."

He was fading away again, but he whispered one more thing just before he lost consciousness, "Boy, you got to ride that bull! It says so in the red part!"

FOURTEEN
Eight Seconds
of Tribulation

"You're not going to ride tonight, are you, Barney?"

Tater and I had been sitting beside Jim Bob all morning and most of the afternoon. He hadn't been conscious long, and it scared me to see how still he lay there.

I looked over at Tater and said, "Why not?"

"Well, he might wake up or something."

To tell the truth, I'd been trying to think of an excuse for staying off one of those bulls, and I almost grabbed at this one, but then I didn't.

"I won't be gone long." I gave an imitation of a cheerful smile, but Tater knew how it was. "Only takes eight seconds to win, you know. A guy ought to be able to stand eight seconds of just about anything, shouldn't he?"

She just shook her head and put her small hand on Jim Bob's arm. He was under one of those clear plastic oxygen tents, and his breathing was shallow.

"Barney, don't go. I–I'm afraid to stay here alone!"

I opened my mouth to surrender, but just then Jim Bob gave a sigh and opened his eyes. He took a look around, then spotted Tater and me. We both jumped up and leaned over the plastic. "Hey!" he whispered. "What time is it?"

I glanced at my watch and said, "It's almost five o'clock, Jim Bob. You feeling all right?"

He licked his lips and said, "Gimme a drink." Tater lifted the plastic, and he swallowed some water, then lay back and looked at me. "What you doin' here, boy? You're supposed to be at the Coliseum, ain't you?"

"Well, I didn't want to leave you. . . ."

"You get, boy!" There was a flash of the old fire in his eyes that made me glad, and he jabbed his finger at me, saying, "You ain't foolin' me, boy! I know you're scared. Ain't no shame in that. But there's shame in runnin' from the thing you're scared of!"

"Sure, Jim Bob, I know. But I had to find out if you were going to make it. I tried to go help Jack, and—I just *couldn't* make it! I just couldn't! You did, though. You saved Jack's life!"

"And he hasn't even called or come by to say a word of thanks!" Tater said. "What a mean thing he is!"

"Jim Bob, do you know how you got away from that bull?" I asked.

"No. I thought I was a goner."

"Tater just ran out there and pulled him away from you like he was a kitten!"

"Well, ain't that a pretty come-off!" he said with a smile. "Don't want you to do that ever again, but Texas gals, why, they jest can't be pushed, can they now?" He paused as if to catch his breath. "Boy, go ride that critter! I'd rather see you stomped than scared!"

"I think you got that right," I said slowly. "Tater, aren't you going? The barrel riding events will start early, I think."

"I better stay with Jim Bob."

"Both of you get outta here. . . ." He shook his head as we tried to argue, then closed his eyes. "Best medicine for ole Jim Bob Puckett would be to wake up and find out that you two younguns did yourself proud."

He seemed to grow limp, and I pulled Tater out into the hall. "Let's go. We can take a cab to the Coliseum."

We got there in time to eat some burgers, which I didn't really want. Then we found Debra grooming her horse, and she was nervous as a cat.

"Look at my hand, Barney!" she cried. "I'm shaking like a leaf!" She bit her lip and said, "I'll probably fall off and break my neck! How's Jim Bob?"

"Well, he woke up just before we left. Looks bad, but I'm praying hard!" Joe and

Jake showed up then, and we helped the girls get their horses ready and in place. Instead of going up into the stands, we watched from the pens.

Debra was the fourth contestant, and if she was nervous, she sure didn't show it! She shot around those barrels like a comet, scraping a couple, but they didn't fall. Her time was a couple of seconds better than the first two riders, and she fell off her horse laughing with excitement.

"You did great!" I told her. Then we stood together and watched the other girls. They all did well, except for one chubby blonde who managed to knock every barrel over, then fell off her horse in the process!

Finally, the announcer said, "And now, Miss Tater Crockett on Don Pedro!"

Well, she did fine—for a girl with so little experience. You could tell that she had lots of ability, but she was too eager and knocked the last barrel over. You hardly ever finish in the money when you do that, and I was afraid she was going to be awfully disappointed.

She wasn't, though. She got off Don Pedro and stroked his nose, saying, "It was *my* fault, not yours!"

"You did so *well*, Tater!" Debra said, giving her a big hug. "Next year you'll retire us all!"

I hugged her, too. "Good ride!"

She smiled shyly at us, then hugged us both and said, "Even if I don't get to keep

Don Pedro, I'm not alone anymore! I got real friends!"

Just then I heard the words I'd been dreading, "And now, folks, here it comes— bull riding! Hold on to your Stetsons!"

I jerked as if I'd grabbed a hot wire, and both girls noticed it. "Guess I better mosey over to the chutes," I said, trying to sound like a real tough guy. The only trouble was that my throat was so dry my voice broke right in the middle of it, which hardly sounded tough!

Debra suddenly hugged me and gave me a big kiss right on the cheek. "Barney, you're a top hand with me, no matter what happens!"

"Me, too!" Tater said and planted a kiss on the other cheek.

I grinned at them. "What is this power I have over women? I must use it only for good!"

I left them and found Jake, Joe, and Judd waiting to help me get on. None of them had the faintest idea of how to do that. I think Joe would have put me on *backward* if I hadn't insisted on facing forward.

Judd had something on his mind. I could see he hated the whole thing, but then cars were about all he did like. He stared at the mangy bull named Tribulation I'd drawn and said, "I been talking to some of these guys, Barney. You know what they all say?"

"What, Judd?"

"Why, this bull ain't *never* been rode!" He

189

stared at Tribulation with a wild look on his face. "Barney, he's stomped a bunch of guys! I ain't kidding! That's what they all say!"

"I know the bull," I said.

And I did. As Jim Bob had said, some bulls just never do get ridden to a finish, and Jim Bob said that this particular bull was the worst in the country in the high school circuit.

Joe grabbed my shoulder and he was pale as a ghost. "Barney, Jake and me have been listening to the riders. They all say this bull is a killer!"

"Barney, we don't need the money," Jake said. "I don't want you to ride this monster!"

Up until then I was walking and talking, but it was a big act! Inside, I was so scared it was pitiful! And all the time I was planning to do whatever I had to do to stay off that bull. I was going to pretend to be sick. Or I was going to spur the bull in the chute so that he couldn't be handled. Anything to stay off of him!

Then a strange thing happened. I still don't understand it myself, and I don't expect anybody else to understand it either.

As soon as I heard that I was up to ride Tribulation, all the fear just left! I think that as long as I had *hope*, I was ready to do anything to keep it. When I knew that I was going to be on a bull that nobody had ever ridden, what hope was there in *that?* When I looked at Tribulation, the fear was all gone. I knew with my mind that in a few seconds I'd be on the ground with that beast trying to stomp me to death, but for some crazy reason it didn't send me off into a screaming fit.

I had a root canal done once, and the dentist had told me that's just about the most painful thing that a guy can have. He said he was going to give me nitrous oxide—what some people call laughing gas. Well, it was the strangest thing. The tooth still hurt when the dentist worked on it, and I knew what was going on all the time, but I just didn't care. It was as if I were watching the dentist grind on somebody else. I remember thinking, *That certainly does hurt!* But it was as if somebody else were getting hurt and I was just an interested observer.

That's what it was like as I got up over Tribulation and settled down onto his broad back. I was thinking, *I'm going to get stomped, by George.* But it was like saying that somebody in China was going to get hurt. Nothing to do with me.

Psychologists would probably have an explanation—that maybe it was just some sort of mental state. But I thought that God was taking care of me, and I still do!

Anyway, I eased down and got the rope in place, then looked up and gave the guys a wink. The chute opened and out we went!

Tribulation didn't *seem* as bad as some

other bulls I'd seen or even ridden. He was rough—strong and able to change directions before you were ready. Then just as I was thinking that maybe I *could* stay on, he went on after-burners! He seemed to be on ball bearings, going in two or three directions at once! Up, down, whipping to the side, twisting and plunging—he did it all.

I felt myself slipping off, and tried to pull myself back to center, but he'd felt me going and did a little slip and slide he probably kept for special occasions. Then I was off and rolling in the dust!

I wasn't hurt, but if I didn't get out of Tribulation's way, I soon would be! He came for me like I was his midnight snack, but the clown picked him up, and I scrambled through the bars and stood there gasping for breath.

The whole bunch hit me then, hollering and beating me the way people do at ball games when their guys win. "You did it! You did it!" they were all screaming.

I called out, "Well, I'm in one piece, and if the Lord can get me through Tribulation, why he can get me through anything. Even if it was a bum ride. . . ."

"Bum ride!" Debra yelled. "Bum ride, my foot! You rode Tribulation! Didn't you hear the buzzer! You're the first cowboy to ever stay on him!"

Then I heard the crowd, and they were going wild! The announcer was saying, "Get that young man out here!" A bunch of guys caught me and the first thing I knew I was standing out in the open with a guy shoving a microphone at me, asking, "How does it feel, cowboy? How'd you do it?"

I'd had trouble giving a speech in a class of twenty kids I knew. When I looked around at the sea of faces, I nearly passed out! But I knew I had to say something.

"Well, I'm just a beginner. Lots of riders right here who can beat me. But there's a man named Jim Bob Puckett who helped me. So all I have to say is, thanks to the Good Lord and Jim Bob Puckett, I made that ride!" There was a lot of clapping as I got away, but the look I got from Tater and Debra and Jake and Joe meant a lot more to me than all that applause!

Jim Bob had to stay in the hospital for a couple weeks, but we went and got him when the doctor said he could leave.

He was still pretty weak, but he perked up a lot when he got home.

Mrs. Simpkins loved taking care of invalids, and she babied him something awful!

On the second day he was home he made me tell him about Don Pedro.

"Well, we didn't get enough prize money to pay for him. So Mr. Dillard came over and took him back," I explained.

Jim Bob got red in the face. "Danged horse thief! I shoulda been here!" Then he shook his head and said, "I sure did let that Texas gal down, didn't I now?"

"Don't worry," I said. "Tater's doing *great!* You know, I'm sorry she had to lose the horse, but out of all this she found out that she's not alone, you know?"

He stared across the yard at the hills, then nodded. "Been finding out about that myself, boy. Always been a loner, but that's no good!"

"Well, you're not now!" I laughed. "You got Bucks and Crocketts running out of your ears!"

He pulled the battered Bible out of his pocket and said, "You know what I found here, boy? Says, 'Two are better than one— woe to him that is alone when he falleth; for he hath not another to help him up.' " He closed the Bible, then smiled at me. "Guess you got to me jest in time, boy! I was like that—fallin' and not a soul to care. Sad to think how many folks like that there is in this world."

"Sure is."

We talked a lot those first few days, and the Crocketts were over every day along with a lot of other people.

We got into the habit of making a big freezer of homemade ice cream every afternoon. Jim Bob wouldn't let us put anything in it—not even peaches or bananas. "It ain't *natural!*" he snapped. "The Lord intended for us to eat plain vanilla ice cream.

Anybody who messes up on good vanilla ice cream is a communist!"

We were all laughing one afternoon just about dark, when suddenly Jim Bob said in a whisper, "Well, lookee here!"

We all looked up to see Jack Monroe riding out of the woody road that lead to the clearing where the house was! He was riding Don Pedro!

"He's got a crust!" Judd growled. "Never even called to find out if Jim Bob was alive or dead—and after Jim Bob saved his worthless hide!"

"Can I hit him with a rock?" Jake asked.

"Quiet!" I said. Then I got up and walked out to meet him. "Hello, Jack. Good to see you."

Debra had followed behind me. "Come on and have some ice cream, Jack."

He looked nervous, and his face was moving as if he were having some kind of attack. He started to say something, then stopped. He was staring at Jim Bob, who'd walked over to the edge of the porch and was quietly watching him.

Jack seemed to take a grip on himself and finally said, "I–I would have come over to find out how you were, but I–I. . . ."

When Jim Bob saw he was bogged down, he said, "Come on and sit, Jack."

"No. I just came to say—well, I came to say thanks for pullin' that bull off me!"

It was probably the first time in his life he'd ever thanked anyone, but he made it.

"You'd a done the same for me," Jim Bob said smiling.

Jack shook his head. "No, I wouldn't. And I can't figure out why you did it, but I sure am glad you did."

Everyone got sort of quiet, and then my brother Jake said in a loud voice, "Well, I think you got rotten manners, Jack Monroe! No, don't shush me!" he said as Tater tried to get him to be quiet. "There you are riding that horse over here, when you know how Tater loved him. You just got no class!"

Jack didn't get angry, as I expected him to. He grinned and said, "You Bucks are all alike—too quick on the trigger! But I got the best of you this time!"

"How's that, Jack?"

"Why, that fool uncle of mine, he took it on himself to come after this horse! I didn't tell him to do it." Then Jack dipped his head and added, "Course, I ain't proud of the way I've acted. But maybe this will do a little to make up for it."

He reached into his pocket and pulled out a piece of paper. "There, Tater. You got yourself a horse!"

Tater stared at the paper, and then Jim Bob took it from her. "You're givin' Don Pedro to Tater?" he asked, and there was a warm smile on his face.

"Oh, you folks paid all but a few hundred on him anyway," Jack muttered. "That skinflint uncle of mine won't miss it!"

"Oh, boy!" Tater yelled and made a beeline for Don Pedro. She was petting his nose and calling him baby names and all that stuff.

I said, "That's real fine, Jack."

Then he got all red and spit over the rail and hung his thumbs in his belt. "Guess you think I'm a prodigal son, or maybe that I've got religion! Well, I'm just tryin' to do what's *right!* So I've done it and I'm goin' home."

He stopped to shake hands with Jim Bob and said, "Well, thanks again."

"Sure," Jim Bob said, and that was all, but I knew it was a big thing.

Jack turned to go, but Tater said, "Why, you can't walk all the way back to your house! Come on. We'll ride double. Then I can ride Don Pedro back."

Jack laughed and said, "No, thanks! I nearly got a chair broke over my head the last time we went out, Tater."

She blushed. Then Jim Bob said, "Why, this will be different. You jest go right on. We trust you, Jack!"

Jack didn't see the wink he gave me, and he said, "Well, thanks, Jim Bob. It's good to see you trust me."

He got on and Tater got on behind him and they rode Don Pedro out of the yard toward his place.

"You gonna let them do that?" Judd demanded.

"Sure, but we'll go give 'em a little close surveillance!" Jim Bob said with a wink. We used Judd's car and my pickup to hold all of us. We caught up with Jack and Tater just as they got to the highway. Then Judd pulled up in front of them with his car loaded with a bunch of Crocketts and Jim Bob. I had Debra in the front seat with me, and Jake and Joe were in the back. Jake had a spotlight we used for going froggin', and Joe had a bull horn that Chief had left for him to fix.

Jack nearly jumped off the horse when we pinned him in!

"Hey, what is this!" he shouted. Jake turned the spotlight right in his face, and Joe bellowed through the loudspeaker, "You are being watched! Jack, no unusual moves!"

I leaned out the window and said, "Just go right along, Jack. We'll be close in case you want anything."

Jack's jaw dropped open and he stared at us. Then he burst out laughing. "All right! But I'll get you guys for this."

He did, too. He waited for his chance, then turned Don Pedro into an opening in the woods and left us there in our vehicles, not able to do a thing.

"Joke's on us, I guess!" I said to Debra.

"They'll be all right," she said.

"I dunno, Debra. Jack's a smooth operator,

and Tater's made one mistake with him already."

"She's grown up, Barney. Don't worry."

"Well, I don't think. . . ."

"Barney, I've got something for you."

"What? For me? Why, it's not my birthday."

"No, but I just want you to have it. It's for both of us, really, something to share."

"Yeah? What is it?"

"Before I give it to you, Barney, will you please tell me how you feel about me?"

Well, a girl is like that. Even Debra had to be told about ten million times that I liked her and that she looked nice and all that stuff.

But I was determined to wean Debra from all that garbage. "Debra, I'm not going to play that game with you. We don't need that sort of stuff. So just forget it!"

That was a little rough, but it was for her own good. You have to be firm with girls. If you ever let them get out of hand, you're in trouble.

Then Debra tapped her chin with her finger and said, "Hmmmmm." Which always made me nervous! She rummaged in her pocket and took out something. "Here's your present, Barney," she said matter-of-factly.

"Debra, it's one of those keen little tape recorders! I always wanted one of those! Hey, thanks a lot!"

I reached out for it, but she pulled it back.

"No, the recorder's not for you. The *tape* is your present."

"The tape? What tape?"

"I'll play it for you," she said, snapping it on.

". . . I love you, Debra," my voice was saying! It was that crazy speech I'd made over the radio.

"You don't have to say nice things to me, Barney," Debra said, snuggling up close to me. "We have it all on tape," she whispered, "and we're going to listen to it all the time! Won't that be nice? Of course," she said, "if you ever get tired of listening to it, why you can always just *tell* me all about how you feel about me."

She had me! I couldn't *stand* to hear that tape and she knew it.

I glared at her. "Debra, you are a very spoiled girl, and. . . ."

She turned the volume up, and I said loudly, "No! No! Don't play that thing!"

She turned it down at once and said with a satisfied smile, "I knew you'd rather tell me with your own lips, Barney. Now, go ahead. And be very specific!"

Well, what could a guy do in a case like that?

I talked until I was tired, and every time I stopped, she turned the dratted thing on!

That bull named Tribulation was *nothing* compared with Debra Simmons!

But all the time I was saying all those

syrupy things, I was making up my mind that I'd get the best of that fool girl if it took me a lifetime to do it!

Well, I could think of worse ways to spend a lifetime.